W9-CIG-086

DON'T MONKEY WITH MURDER

'My Irma has been kidnapped away and I am been in anxiety for her life' ran the ungrammatical line in the letter which brought Mr Dyke and his companion to East Leat, a lovely village lost in the Downs.

But Irma had suffered a fate worse than abduction. She had been stabbed through the heart. The distorted body—black, hairy and bloody—was that of a young chimpanzee.

The whim of an heiress had drawn renowned psychobiologist Dr Paul Virag from the calm of his experimental station in Tobago to chaperon two prized monkeys, Irma and Leofric, across the Atlantic. He was furious at the interruption to his work—and he would have been more furious still if he'd realised what a sinister turn events were about to take.

DON'T MONKEY
WITH MURDER

Elizabeth Ferrars

First published 1942
by
Hodder & Stoughton Ltd

This edition 2007 by BBC Audiobooks Ltd
published by arrangement with
Peter Mactaggart

ISBN 978 1 405 68574 0

British Library Cataloguing in Publication Data available

Printed and bound in Great Britain by
Antony Rowe Ltd., Chippenham, Wiltshire

— I —

I ADMIT IT—I made a great many mistakes in that affair at East Leat. But about one thing I was right, or, rather, about one person.

I was absolutely right about Rosa Miall.

I saw her only once, I never exchanged a single word with her, but I was right that it was Rosa Miall who dominated the whole unpleasant business from beginning to end. That it was in the pattern of her curious mind, in the dire efficiency of her conscience, in the strength and definiteness of her personality that the solutions of most of the questions we had to ask ourselves were to be found, was something that stared at me out of the tangle of evidence as uncompromisingly as she herself might have done. It was because Rosa Miall existed, and that she was what she was, and that she affected other people as she did, that bloody murder ever came to East Leat—at any rate, that particular bloody murder.

East Leat is a village, lovely and lost, in the Downs. The best way to reach it is on foot. The next best way is by car. If you happen to be in a hurry and if you happen not to have been able to pay the tax and insurance on your car, the only thing to do is to take the train to Bule. It means changing at Changley and Ashingham, and takes at least five hours. Not many people have the stamina to attempt it. I remember that when the seven-three stopped at Bule that Friday evening, only four others besides George and myself got out of the train.

One, probably a farmer's wife, laden with parcels and with the slightly riotous look on her face that can only be engendered by tea and cream-cakes, was obviously returning from a day's shopping in Ashingham. One was a schoolboy, one was a business-man, one was an elderly lady of the type that goes vigorously dressed in tweeds and makes or breaks the vicar. All four seemed to be so well known to the solitary porter that he did not even look up from watering a bed of love-lies-bleeding up against the station railings to relieve them of their tickets.

George and I went as far as the empty booking-office. We saw the farmer's wife climb into a bus and be carried off in it, the business-man get into a waiting car, the schoolboy stroll off whistling, while the lady in tweeds signalled a decrepit vehicle standing in the station yard and was driven away. The porter made up his mind not to worry about George and me and went on with his watering.

It was a fine summer evening. The slant of the sunlight left long shadows of church-spire, roof and tree across the ground. There were low, green hills close at hand. Bule itself consisted of only a handful of houses, a church, a couple of shops, a couple of chapels and a small, squat inn which, in large letters of tarnished gold, advertised the fact that it sold Nutlin's beers. There were few people about, and once the creaking taxi with the elderly lady in it had disappeared, there was no traffic at all but a child on a little wooden tricycle pedalling his way up the middle of the road. There were some poppies growing out of a crack in the wall, there was thick, white dust in the road, and a thick, white coating of dust on the chestnut trees, the grass of the village green and the hawthorn hedges.

I had been very unwilling to make this trip to East Leat; it was George who had insisted on our coming, talking at me for most of the morning about my bank-balance. Now, as the minutes passed and no one came to meet us, I began to air the fact that I had a grievance. That Bule, cupped in its hills, was a place of charm, that there was a sweet country peace about the grey stone houses and the gardens ablaze with the flowers of June, meant very little to me. Each person who passed at a distance I stared at with a growing feeling of resentment; not one of them could possibly have been taken for a foreigner—a foreigner in desperate need of help to save a daughter from kidnapping.

For that, as I understood the letter from the man who had signed himself Paul Virag, was why we were wanted.

The letter had reached me that morning. Addressed in a spidery, foreign handwriting, it had had the word URGENT, in large, excitable capital letters, written in one corner. At the top of the letter had been written: " c/o Miss Rosa Miall,

2 Titmore Lane, East Leat, nr Bule." The letter had run:

"DEAR SIR,

Before this you shall have heard from Professor Potter, whom I see last Wednesday, of my trouble what I am in. My Irma has been kidnapped away and I am been in anxiety for her life. By her own intelligence alone is she come back, the police giving hindering as much as help, saying such things are not occurring in this country. I say it is occurred now two times. But I think they are not liking me much for being a foreigner. So I beg you to come to my help and greatly oblige me. I will pay whatever is usual fee in such occasions and all reasonable expenses. There is a train which arrives at Bule Station at seven-three which on Friday I shall meet and hope to find you. I explain all else at that juncture. I am, sir, sending you my kindest regards and best wishes,

PAUL VIRAG."

Now in the dusty booking-office, after five hours of waiting in sidings, of shunting and changing trains, of sultry heat and a headache, I was not in a mood to take the absence of Paul Virag in a generous spirit. George seemed undisturbed by it, but now and then as we stood there I noticed with satisfaction that he gave me a glance of uneasiness.

Presently I said: "Our return-tickets cost us fifteen and twopence each, George."

He answered: "I reckon that's right, Toby."

"That comes to one pound, ten shillings and four-pence," I said.

"That's right," he agreed.

"That's one pound, ten shillings and fourpence *wasted*."

George said nothing.

Just then a figure appeared round the bend in the road, a tall, slow-moving figure.

However, on approaching it turned out to be nothing but a trudging farmhand in corduroys and one of those bowler hats that can only be bought in places like Bule. I grew more restive than ever and George avoided my eye.

Presently we walked back on to the platform.

The porter was still watering his flowers. The wet earth smelt fresh and cool, the spray from the water-ing-can curved in a glistening shower over the funereal tassels of the love-lies-bleeding.

He gave a start when he heard me clear my throat behind him.

With that feeling of querulous helplessness that descends on people who have come to the ends of the earth in answer to an invitation and have not been met, I demanded: "This *is* Bule station, isn't it?"

The porter nodded at a painted board. "Ay, 'tis Bule for East Leat all right."

"Bule for East Leat all right—and that was the seven-three all right—and it's us all right. But it looks as if nothing else was all right. How far away is East Leat?"

"We-ell," he said, "'tis a goodish step."

"How much of a step?"

9

"Matter of seven mile or so."

I groaned peevishly.

George suggested: "Maybe there's a bus."

We both eyed the porter.

He stooped and pulled a weed out of the flower-bed. Dropping it on to the railway-line he answered slowly: "Ay, there *is* a bus, only . . ."

"Only what?"

"Last bus 'as gorn."

There was a silence.

I think my way of looking at him suggested that I put the blame on him, because he went on soothingly: "Only just gorn. Maybe if you'd made haste when you got out o' the train, you'd a caught'n."

Turning away, I said grimly to George: "Seems like we'll have to take a taxi. It'll bust us, but there's nothing else to do. I'm not going to walk seven miles carrying a suitcase."

The porter coughed gently.

We looked at him.

"Taxi's gorn," he said.

"The trouble is," I said bitterly, "we townsfolk are obviously too slow for this country hustle. We're too slow to catch the last bus, and too slow to collar the only taxi, and for all we know, we've been too slow for Paul Virag. He may have been here at seven-three and found he just couldn't stand the strain of waiting while we got out of the train and got our bearings. I expect he drove off home while we were dawdling along the platform. And now if we go over to that revolting-looking pub opposite and ask if they can do us a dinner of some sort, they'll tell us we're too late for that too."

"Ay," said the porter, "I reckon you be. They does high teas, but they wouldn't expect anyone to expect high tea as late as this, now would they?"

Giving him a blank, antagonistic stare, I walked away. George picked up the two suitcases and followed.

Once more we stood in the road outside the station.

In the dust near the door of the inn a yellow cat lay stretched on its side in the sunshine. It looked pleased with itself and its circumstances. Raising its head, it licked lazily at its fur. As its eyes dwelt on us for a moment, I could have sworn they filled with indolent mockery.

George put down the suitcases.

"You know, Tobe," he said, "that man Virag ain't so very late yet. Maybe, if we was just to wait a bit longer, he'd turn up."

I was looking at the yellow cat.

"Seven miles!" I said balefully.

"Suppose we was to try telephonin'?" said George. "Then they can tell us what's gone wrong."

It was an idea, anyway.

I went into the oddly new-looking kiosk outside the station and hunted in the directory for Rosa Miall's telephone-number. But it was useless; apparently she didn't believe in the telephone.

George, taking a look at my face as I came out again, said hurriedly: "Tobe, I got another idea. I was thinkin' maybe if we was to wait over there in the pub—and even if they can't do us a meal they'll be able to do us a glass of bitter—if we was to wait over there we could see him if he did happen to turn up."

" He won't turn up," I said. " All along I've been feeling there was something wrong about that letter. I said it right away, didn't I? I said there was something wrong about a man who mentions that he's willing to pay all 'reasonable expenses.' Because it isn't likely, is it, that I'm going to turn up at East Leat near Bule or anywhere else, unless he pays all reasonable expenses—and a bit more? So it's only unreasonable expenses that would have been worth mentioning."

" But he may still turn up, Tobe."

" Oh, you're no sort of a psychologist, George. A man who talks about 'reasonable expenses' has a slow, plodding, precise sort of mind. He's the sort of man who always turns up on the dot. And so the fact that he wasn't here at seven-three means he isn't going to turn up at all."

" All the same, if he did happen to turn up, the pub's the place he'd come and look for us, isn't it? "

" Unless the Y.M.C.A. was as far as his imagination took him." However, I picked up one of the suitcases and walked towards the Station Hotel.

It was a shadowy, dusty place with a bar—small, dark and empty. On the walls there were a surprising number of advertisements for non-alcoholic beverages, all decorated with pictures of young ladies with the concealed foreheads and brief tunics of the nineteen-twenties. There were warnings against betting. The lace curtains over the windows were tied with dusty, velvet bows. In a glass case above the mantelpiece was a stuffed fox with a partridge in its mouth. Fox and partridge both looked as if moths had long since had their way with them; only the red paint splashed over the fox's jaws had an appearance of astonishing, gory freshness.

After my second, or it may have been my third, pint of Nutlin's beer, I drew the attention of the barmaid to this ornament. A stout, prim-looking woman, she kept popping out to serve us through a small doorway at the back of the bar, like an elderly rabbit popping out of a dark, smelly burrow.

"That's very beautiful blood on that fox's teeth," I said. "D'you freshen it up from time to time?"

She stared at it.

Outside the shadows had shifted and the yellow cat, overtaken by them, had got up and stretched itself in a new patch of sunshine. The child on the tricycle had been called indoors by its mother.

"No," said the woman, after some thought, "we don't. I don't know why we should want to do a thing like that."

"I just thought perhaps you did," I said.

"No," she said, "we don't. It stays nice and bright like that of itself."

"How nice," I said.

"I reckon it is," she said.

"Isn't it?" I said.

"Yes, it is," she said.

I said to George: "I can't take much more of this sitting down. I'm going to walk around a bit. I'll be back soon."

I plunged out into the street, nearly falling over

the yellow cat, which chose that moment to change its mind about the best patch of the receding sunshine.

I strolled around the village for some time. I found to my surprise that it possessed a cinema; it was in a converted barn and it opened twice a week. I did not recognise the names of any of the films it advertised as coming shortly, though something about their titles haunted me like a scent or a sound suddenly recaptured from a forgotten childhood. There was a grocer's shop which was also a post-office, and a chemist's and ironmonger's combined. On a drinking-trough there were faded placards about foot-and-mouth disease and Colorado beetles. There was also an undertaker's; in his window, between two modest marble urns, there was a photograph of a hearse, and beneath it the inscription: " This hearse cannot be converted into a landaulette."

I made my way back to the hotel again.

I said, slumping down on a stool: " It seems there's nowhere but this frowsy dungeon to get a night's rest in except the churchyard, so there's only one thing to do—we'll catch the next train back to London."

With a slight, regretful shake of the head George said: " Last train's gone, Tobe."

" What? "

" While you was out there, walkin' around. It come in and gone out. You can bet there won't be another tonight."

As I let my head sink on to my hands the yellow cat slid in over the doorstep. Advancing fastidiously like a proud, skinny dowager, it jumped on to George's stomach, where it immediately started purring away as if it were being paid to do it. My stare, fixed on one of the young ladies whose seductiveness it had once been thought would assist the sales of non-alcoholic apple-juice, grew increasingly vacant. My headache, hunger and depression deadened protest.

I suppose it was the expression on my face that made George, some minutes later, speak to me in the way he did.

" Tobe, I ain't by any means sure," he said, " and now that you look like gettin' resigned to the situation I don't want to raise false hopes in you, but —don't you hear a car? "

" It's that cat," I said. " It's making as much noise as a whole traffic-jam."

" No, it's a car," said George.

" Then it's probably that moth-eaten taxi returning—and you'll find it's got union rules against going out again at this time of night."

" 'Tisn't night, it's scarcely past eight o'clock," said George, " and 'tisn't that taxi."

" You'll see it is," I said.

But I was wrong.

The car, which a moment later was driven rapidly up to the station and jerked to a temperamental standstill by powerful brakes, was a long, cream-coloured saloon—slim, swift and exciting.

The driver was a girl.

As she leapt from the car and went hurrying, almost running, into the station, I had an impression of dark hair, smart clothes, and a swift, warm vitality of movement. In a moment she was back again, standing by the car, looking around her in tense, excitable uncertainty. Putting out a hand to the door of the car, she started to open it, then checked herself, started to open it again, then suddenly slammed it shut. Looking straight at the doorway of the Station Hotel, and with that same taut, nervous haste, she walked swiftly forward.

I let out the breath I had been holding.

"George," I said, "if this is Irma, I'm ready to forgive everybody everything!"

*   *   *   *   *

That was a first impression. Later—I wasn't so sure.

But certainly she was a delightful object to look at. She was about nineteen. She was small and, though she was slenderly shaped, there was a young, luscious plumpness about her. Her light-blue linen dress was very well cut, her make-up was effective. Her dark hair was short, growing low on her forehead in a thick cloud of natural curls. She had a clear, pallid skin and rather high cheekbones. The eyes, set far apart above a small, soft blob of a nose, had long fringes of dark, curling lashes. In those eyes at the moment shone a desperate look of inquiry.

She spoke quickly in the doorway, with glances from one to the other of us: "Please, I am looking for a gentleman called Mr Dyke. Can you tell me anything of where I may find him?" Her voice

16

was a rich one with a not quite English resonance in the vowels.

I had got to my feet. "My name's Dyke," I said.

"Ah," said the girl sombrely, and she did not reply to my smile, "I thought it must be."

"I think you must be Miss Virag," I said.

She nodded briefly. Her glance settled searchingly on George. As he never likes being looked at searchingly, even by someone who has nothing to do with the police, he hurriedly hid his face in his beer-mug. The girl turned back to me.

"You are together?" she asked suspiciously.

"Yes," I said, "we are."

"But I was told only of one gentleman."

"Whereas I've been told relatively nothing," I said. "Anyway, this is George, and we are together."

But she insisted: "I was told only of a Mr Dyke to whom I was to give my father's apologies and to make explanations."

"That's all right," I said, "you can count George in on them both—I'm useless without him."

"In that case," she said, her rich voice still formal and unfriendly, "please will you both come with me? I shall explain as we go. I have to say that my father is very, very grieved at his discourtesy in leaving you here, and he will be most grateful for your having remained instead of returning instantly to London." It was spoken glibly like a lesson. "You will come, please? We should not waste time, we should return to the house as quickly

17

as possible. Only . . . it just occurs to me, perhaps before we start . . ."

She hesitated. Her bright, sullen glance sought mine.

" Yes? " I said helpfully.

" I should like it very much if you would please offer me a drink."

" By all means—of course." I was eyeing her with a good deal of curiosity. " What'd you like? "

" I am very fond of whisky," she said simply.

As I rapped on the bar to attract the stout woman out of her burrow once more, the girl stepped into the room. She leant a white elbow on the bar, and, letting out a long, throaty sigh, she closed her eyes; she managed a very dramatic expression of weariness.

" It has been such an evening, a *terrible* evening! " she said. Then she opened her eyes again and looked around her. " I have never been in an English public-house before."

" Don't judge them all by this one," I warned her. " You haven't been long in England? "

" Only one week."

" You—er, come from . . . ? "

" We came from Tobago, of course."

" Oh—of course." I fished for some money in my pocket to pay for her drink.

She muttered thank-you as I pushed the glass towards her. She took it up quickly.

" Please," she went on, " say nothing about this to my father. Say that I brought you back with me as soon as I found you. You will, please? "

"All right," I said, "if that's how it has to be."

"You really will?" She drank. "You will? You will say nothing?"

"You can rely on me."

"Even if he asks you directly?"

I looked at her dubiously. "Why ever should he do that?"

"Because he's very suspicious of all that I do, and allows me no freedom to enjoy any of the pleasures of life, and never believes what I say."

"Perhaps that's just for your safety at the moment," I said. "I mean, with these kidnappers around——"

She said a rude word vigorously. Then she added: "Please do not mention to him that I know that word—except that his English is very bad, poor man, so perhaps it's of no consequence."

"You haven't explained what went wrong with this evening," I said. "What made it so terrible?"

Her eyebrows flicked together in a frown. "Oh, I shall tell you everything—and then my father will tell you everything—and then Mrs Peach will tell you everything—and then Miss Teed will tell you everything. Oh, I'm so bored—I tell you, Mr Dyke, I'm so bored and distracted with it all. You see, it happened again this afternoon."

"What?"

I stared at her.

"And my father's so stupid about it, he goes right out of his head." She drank some more whisky.

"But d'you mean to say . . .? D'you mean you've just been . . .?" I stopped. I began to feel I had gone wrong somewhere.

It was true she was nervous and on edge, but all the same . . .

She was saying peevishly: "It's so silly to make such a fuss about it. I could scream, the way people go on. I'm the only one who doesn't get upset. But all this excitement and searching and everything—it makes me so irritated."

"Look here," I said, "I'd like to clear up a few things. First, I'd better explain, I'm almost completely in the dark. Professor Potter, whom your father evidently relied on to give me the outlines of the case, never told me anything about it at all —in fact, when I rang him up this morning to make some inquiries, he said he couldn't even remember having met your father, except ten years ago in Buenos Ayres. Potter says he was drunk on Wednesday evening and doesn't remember anything. He added that he always gets drunk in advance when he knows he's got to go out with other scientists."

"Ah," said the girl, "of course my father wouldn't notice it. He never notices anything about people. They aren't his subject, you see."

I didn't exactly, but I went on: "Well then, you can understand, can't you, Miss Virag, that I'm feeling confused? Because if there was really another attempt to kidnap you this evening . . ." I fingered my chin. "The fact is, I feel I must have got hold of the wrong end of the stick somehow. Tell me, isn't your name Irma?"

With a thump she put her glass down. Either the whisky or some sudden emotion brought a flush to her pretty, plump cheeks. Then her shoulders were shaking, her whole small, rather edible-looking body was bouncing up and down on her stool with laughter.

"So you thought Irma was me!"

"Oh," I said, "I see—she isn't."

She went on laughing. But after the first moment of spontaneity there was a disturbing, over-excited sound in her laughter and the tears that gathered in her eyes were the tears of mirth that is half hysterical.

"If it had been me," she said, suddenly grave and with a rasp in her rich voice, "my father would have thought the police quite clever enough to deal with it. It is because it happens to be one of his chimpanzees that heaven and earth have to be moved on account of it."

"Chimpanzees!"

"Of course."

"Of course, of course." I looked at George. He was looking at me and grinning. Both of us at the same moment gave a very slight shake of the head.

The girl saw it. Her voice went satirical: "Haven't you ever heard of Paul Virag—Dr Paul Virag—the psychobiologist?"

"No," I said, "I haven't."

"You ought to have," she said, "if you'd been properly educated."

"Well, I live sort of out of the world—at any rate, out of *that* world."

She explained: "For the last ten years my father has been running an experimental station at Tobago. He's got seventeen chimpanzees there—no, only fifteen now, since he had to bring Irma and Leofric to England. He's been working on the mentality of the chimpanzee all his life."

"So I'm here to look into the attempted theft of a chimpanzee, am I, and not the kidnapping of a cherished daughter?" I burst out laughing.

"Chimpanzees," she said sharply, "are very valuable animals."

"I'll bet they are! But tell me, what's your father doing with them over here? Showing them or something?"

"No," she replied; "he's presenting them to an old lady who happens to want some."

I leant towards her. "Did you say an old lady who happens to want some?"

"Yes," she said.

"Whew!"

As a matter of fact, I admired her; I thought she did it marvellously. But I thought she was too young to be allowed to see that. Drawing a hand across my mouth I managed to wipe the smile off, and said pretty grimly: "That's enough, Miss Virag—that's quite enough. You were doing nicely, and I was almost believing you until you brought in the old lady. But that's overdoing it. No, no, you needn't look upset, we aren't annoyed, George and I—oh no, we've got a sense of humour and we think it very funny. But all the same we're going back to London just as fast as that village hearse that can't be converted into a landaulette, or anything else on wheels we can get hold of, will take us there."

While I was speaking the girl's face went puzzled, then it went frigid, then it went white and violent.

"Do you mean to say you disbelieve what I am telling you?"

"Well, I was sort of carried away by it at first," I said, "but now——"

"Ah, I *hate* people who disbelieve me!" she cried shrilly. "I hate it more than I hate anything! I'm a completely sincere person. I think it's wicked to tell lies; I never tell them. And when people disbelieve me I never forgive them!"

"Oh come, it isn't as serious as all that," I said, "and George and I aren't annoyed about it—at least, not very."

But she gave a sharp shake of her head. "I have very deep feelings about truth and sincerity. I—I think they're sacred things. It's one of the things about my father that I—I can't respect, that he thinks I'm a person who tells lies and behaves untruthfully."

"That's hard," I said; "but George and I can take a joke."

"*But this is the truth!*"

The look of her distorted mouth and blazing eyes worried me.

"All right," I said after a moment, "I believe you."

"You don't," she said.

"I do."

"Oh no, you don't—your tone isn't serious."

"I believe you," I said distinctly, "seriously."

She sighed. "It isn't the words, it's the tone that counts, and yours isn't serious."

I had another try at it, but she only said: "It still doesn't sound right."

George took a hand. He said: "Look here, miss: Toby here, he once had a very nasty experience through believing a young lady, and somehow he got his bump of believing injured, so that it ain't never functioned properly since. You needn't be sorry for him, because that's the way he gets his livin', mostly by doubtin' people. I reckon you'll have heard of those Eastern beggars who get a livin' by showin' off their horrible deformities and who think that a doctor who offers to cure them is tryin' to take their livelihood away. Well, that's how it is with Toby; he don't *want* to be convinced by people."

The girl turned and took another look at George. I don't think he had made much of an impression until then; he is short and pinkly plump, with slick, yellow hair and indefinite features. As she looked at him he dived into his beer-mug again. The girl's face remained sullen, and turning away again she sucked hungrily at the last few drops in her glass.

I said: "What strikes me at the moment is that if we stay here much longer talking like this, your father's going to start wondering where you are and what you're doing, and then, of course, he'll start asking questions, won't he?"

She set her glass down with a rap on the polished wood.

"You are right," she said abruptly. "We must go."

She turned to the door. Her shoulders were straight, her head was high. But in the doorway she faltered for a moment. Her small, plump hands started twisting round one another.

"Of course, you remember your promise not to say anything to my father of my entering a public-house and drinking some whisky. It would make him very angry. In anger he is terrible."

She swept out ahead of us.

George and I exchanged glances, then followed a few paces behind her.

*　　*　　*　　*　　*

Even if I had not yet made up my mind whether or not to believe the girl, with her stories of apes and old ladies, I know that as we got into the car I started wanting to believe her.

I started thinking how interesting it would be to meet the sort of old lady who "happened to want some chimpanzees." I started thinking that to trace a missing ape would be as intriguing and far less harrowing than to trace a missing daughter. At the same time I had a feeling that this nice-looking young girl, with her altogether too passionate defence of her own integrity, was probably one of those people to whom the sharing of a world of fantasy seems much more attractive as a form of conversation than any discussion of sober matters of fact.

The road from Bule to East Leat, which ran at first between hedges and under the deep shadows of old beech trees, climbed steadily towards the Downs. There were foxgloves along the banks and wild roses caught up amongst the hazels. The sky overhead was flecked with patches of pink cloud, while in the west bold streaks of gold were splashed above the scalloped edge of low, green hills.

The girl was silent. Her forehead had puckered into frowning lines. The way the lines came, harsh and straight across the low brow, suggested that habit had already creased them into the skin. When presently I offered her a cigarette she refused with a shake of the head, muttering: "You ought not to have disbelieved me."

I tried to reason with her. "Look here," I said, "if I was wrong just now I'm awfully sorry, but you must be able to see for yourself what a—well, what a funny sort of yarn it makes; I mean the idea of a man coming all the way from Tobago to make a present of two chimpanzees to an old lady. Consider it dispassionately. Don't you think that——?"

She burst out: "But I would never do anything so discourteous as tell you a lie—you, a complete stranger! Why should you think such a thing of me?"

I decided to pour on the oil. "I'm sure you wouldn't, Miss Virag—of course you wouldn't. I realise, I really do, that I must have been completely mistaken. All the same, she must be a pretty rum old lady, mustn't she? "

" Oh, she is! " said the girl quickly. " She's the most extraordinary old lady I ever met. D'you know, she has lots and lots of money, but she won't have any servants? And she runs a club in the village—Dr Glynne told me about it—where she has lecturers to come and tell the village people all about physiology and eugenics and economics and such things. And she belongs to all sorts of societies that want to bring Prohibition to this country. And a few years ago, Miss Teed told me, she took to interfering every time anyone in the village got engaged to be married to anyone else in the village; she said the village was so isolated there was too much inbreeding already and that that was why there was such a lot of mental deficiency. She broke up many marriages, Miss Teed said, before the motor-buses started coming."

I raised an eyebrow. " Motor-buses? "

" Yes, and that was her doing too. She wrote letters to members of parliament and started petitions, and once dug the chairman of the bus company in the stomach with her umbrella so that they should start buses from Bule to East Leat. You see, she thought that if the girls in East Leat could go to the cinema in Bule on their days off, perhaps they'd get married to the boys in Bule, and then there wouldn't be so many mad people in East Leat. But shall I tell you what seems to me the most extraordinary thing she's done? "

"Please," I said. "I should think it'd be worth hearing."

"She's gone away," said the girl.

I was puzzled.

"The moment we arrived," she said, "she went away."

"But d'you mean——?"

"Yes, just what I'm saying. The moment my father and I and Ingham the keeper and Irma and Leofric arrived, she went away—well, not the very same moment exactly, but the next morning."

"Perhaps she didn't like the chimps," I said.

"She didn't say so. At any rate, it was very extraordinary behaviour—so *rude!*"

"Oh, decidedly."

"I should never do such a thing myself."

"I'm sure you wouldn't."

"Of course, I'm glad she went away," said the girl, "it's much nicer without her. She frightened me, she was so dominating. But still, it makes me angry when people are rude to me."

"Who is she, by the way?"

The girl glowered at the road ahead of her.

"She's Miss Rosa Miall, of course."

Flicking some cigarette ash out of the window, I glanced round at George in the back of the car to see how he was taking it. He winked an eye at me.

We had left the hedges behind by now and it was the rough grass of the Downs, scarred here and there with gashes of chalk and dotted with stunted thorn-trees, that stretched away on either side of us. The low, round-shouldered hills were close at hand.

After a moment the girl went on: "I suppose you've never heard of Wilfred Miall? If you've never heard of my father, you won't have heard of Wilfred Miall."

"But I have," I said.

She cried in swift protest: "Why, he's nobody!"

"He's a very rich man."

"But he hasn't done anything. It was always my father who did everything. And Mr Miall knew it; he never pretended to be anyone himself. If you've never heard of my father I don't see why you should have heard of Wilfred Miall."

"People are often heard of simply for being rich."

"How absurd. I shouldn't remember a person's name only because someone said he was rich."

"Where does Wilfred Miall come into the story, anyway?"

"He doesn't," she said.

I was watching her face and noticed how her soft, full lips folded tightly against one another.

"But then——"

She snapped: "He's dead."

As soon as she had said it, I remembered.

The seventy-year-old philanthropist had come to the end of his worthy existence by falling off a bicycle about a year before; I had read a paragraph about it. The reason why the fact had not impressed itself more firmly on my memory was probably that the accident had happened on the same day as one of Hitler's more troublesome utterances.

I said: "Of course. . . . And wasn't there something surprising about his will?"

"There was," she said. "There wasn't one."

At that moment George leant forward and prodded me. When I looked round he jerked a thumb at the hillside. There was a man there, about a hundred yards away. He was waving; against the grey-green background of grass and chalk he was flinging his arms and legs into positions as angularly surprising as those of the twisted thorn trees. I thought that I caught the sound of a shout.

I said: "I say, Miss Virag——"

She looked round. Then she ground on the brakes and the big car stopped with a startled squeal. I saw, for an instant, the sudden intensification of the scowl on her face, and caught the sound of her breath escaping slowly from between clenched teeth. Then, as her hands dropped from the wheel to her lap, she produced a smile. It was a silly, little, meaningless smile. Softly, in an expressionless voice, she murmured: "Thank you, I did not see him. It is my father."

Trotting on heavy feet across the broken ground, the man who had waved to us from the hillside approached the car.

The first thing that came into my mind when I saw Paul Virag was a question. Why did this daughter of his appear to be afraid of him—or to hate him? There was nothing to fear or to hate in that face. It was a strange face; it had the strangeness of unquestionable beauty. Beauty may be an odd word to use about a man of fifty with close-cropped hair going grizzled and a stocky body which, without being fat, had a liberal covering of flesh, a man whose arms were uncommonly short and who carried them away from his sides as if he needed them, as a child does, for balancing. But in the strong, regular features and the nobly modelled head, in the keen blue eyes under level, dark brows, in the vivid intelligence and openness of his expression, there was the kind of rather abstract perfection which can cause complete strangers of both sexes to stare in a sort of surprise.

As George and I made signs of getting out of the car to greet him, Virag waved at us not to stir, and wrenching open a door, flung himself in beside us.

Still panting, he introduced himself and shook hands with us both.

Then he said: "Forgive . . . I was should be at station . . . gravest apologies. But events of this evening are not to have been expected. They are gone—both are gone. I came here searching for them on a false information."

I said: "You mean both—er—chimpanzees have been stolen?"

"Both!" he echoed. "Both—Irma and Leofric. Leofric is most gifted animal I am ever knowing and Irma is affectionate, trustful, very good. They are gone since six o'clock. The cages are open, empty. We seek all the time and telephone, and a man on a bicycle say he have seen an animal here on the hill, but it is nonsense, it is one of those little thorn trees he see. Marti, drive back —it is hopeless, they are gone. The police will be like last time and say I shall keep my cages shut. Shut!" His voice rose angrily. "I shall keep my cages shut, shall I? I have them shut and bolted and locked and padlocked, and Ingham is watching them. But in the one moment when he do not watch the animals are stolen from me. But the police they will say I shall keep my cages shut!" Controlling his voice again, he added quietly: "I am sorry to have disturb you two gentlemen with coming when my animals are gone and they are no more there for you to save them."

The girl started the car again. She did it jerkily and nervously, and I could have sworn that there was apprehension on her face.

I said, studying the scientist's remarkable features: "Perhaps if they aren't there to be protected, they're somewhere for us to find, Dr Virag."

"They are lost," he said; "we are not finding them again."

"It's early to say that, isn't it?"

He looked me in the eyes. I realised the amount of mental energy this man could put into feeling depression and bitterness. "All is against me," he answered harshly. "Since Wilfred die nothing is going right. We are not finding them again—I am sorry you have your journey."

"But look here," I said, not liking his insistence on our presence being useless, "you can't go mislaying things like chimpanzees and then do nothing about it. People won't like it at all. You've got to look for them."

"I look all evening."

"Say," said George, "the Mona Lisa was missin' a lot longer than an evenin', but they got it back."

Virag shook his head. "There is spite and conspiracy against me. I understand now—if I get them back they go again. Very well, I give up, I give up all hope. I go to America and become a professor."

The car, driven fast, was now descending the long, straight road into another valley. But this was not another verdant valley like that in which Bule had been built. Here and there the grass had been replaced by patches of cultivation and there were one or two cottages, but except for these and a wood of beech trees on a hillside ahead, there was only the grey-green quiet of the dry, chalky downland.

I said: "Well, I know a good many people who wouldn't consider it the end of all hope to go to America and become a professor, but if that's how you feel about it, I don't see why you should resign yourself to it until George and I have had a good hunt for your beasts."

"Thank you," said Virag gravely, "I am grateful. But it is useless. You must not waste your time for me. A man's time is precious—or it should be."

"Er—quite so. All the same," I said, "since I'm here——"

"You will waste your time, Mr Dyke."

"But since I *am* here, and since there are some things that I've got pretty confused, perhaps you'd explain them to me. Then I could give you a genuine opinion on whether there's anything I can do for you or not."

"By all means, by all means, if you desire it." He leant back in his seat. "You tell me what you do not understand, I explain." But he sighed. There was a fallen-in look about his face, a brooding weariness.

I said: "I'd like first to know why you're here in England. Then I'd like to know why you've brought two chimpanzees with you. Then I'd like to know what Miss Rosa Miall wants with them, and I'd like to know how the late Wilfred Miall comes into it."

"I see, you want to know everything." He sat considering the questions, ordering them in his mind before he dealt with them. But suddenly, with a gesture of irritation, he exclaimed: "This language—it is to be helpless like a child to speak so little of a language! Do you speak French or German or Italian?"

"Not so's you'd notice," I said.

"Very well, Marti shall explain." He spoke to the girl: "Please, Marti, talk for me and explain what these gentlemen will know. I understand good, but I have no words for myself."

"Yes, papa," she said with soft docility. "I was just about to explain when we saw you waving on the hill. Where shall I begin?"

Virag pondered. "With Wilfred and his money."

34

She slowed the car down a little. She looked round at me.

" You see, Mr Dyke, it was always Mr Miall who financed my father. Father never had any money. It was he who directed all the work at the experimental station, but it was Mr Miall who supplied all the money. Father couldn't have kept going for six months without Mr Miall."

" Six months? Six weeks! " cried Virag.

" Yes, papa—six weeks. But Mr Miall always said father needn't worry about money. He promised to leave him enough in his will to carry on with the work. And father never did worry or think of the future; he trusted Mr Miall completely. And then Mr Miall died and it turned out he had never made a will at all."

" Oh—so that his money went to his next-of-kin? "

" Yes, his sister," muttered Virag, beating the knuckles of his two hands together. " Miss Rosa Miall—she inherit everything."

" My father wrote to her," Marti Virag went on, " and told her about how Mr Miall had always promised him enough money to keep the experimental station going, and suggested to her that she might like to do something about it in memory of her brother. He said he'd name it the Wilfred Miall Experimental Station——"

" The Wilfred de Winter Miall Experimental Station," her father corrected her. " I put his full name in."

" Yes, papa—and then, Mr Dyke, we waited. I,

35

for one, never expected a reply, because why should one give a lot of money away to a lot of strange chimpanzees? That is something I don't understand. And when four or five months had gone by, father was saying too that he didn't think Miss Miall was going to take any notice of his letter. He had been borrowing money and was in debt—we were at our wits' end, Mr Dyke. And then one day there came a letter from Miss Miall, saying she was quite willing to let my father have the money he wanted, provided first that he called his place the Rosa and Wilfred de Winter Miall Experimental Station, and—oh, it was such a ridiculous thing to ask, my father was furious about it—provided he let her have two chimpanzees."

" But in heaven's name, why? "

" She didn't say why."

Here Paul Virag, bouncing in his seat, broke in uncontrollably: " Two of my chimpanzees—*two* of them—for an old woman, an old, mad woman! Tell him, Marti, tell him what I do! "

" Yes, papa. First, Mr Dyke, he called her all the names he could think of—in many languages. Then he wrote her a letter, very stiff and courteous, suggesting that chimpanzees didn't really make suitable pets for elderly ladies, and also that they were very valuable animals and of much greater use to him than they could be to her. This time she answered immediately. She wrote that she was very interested in everything connected with her brother's work, and in the mentality of animals, and——"

"And that she had once had a dog that could count up to twelve!" shouted Virag.

"Yes," said Marti, "and that all the same she didn't feel sure she could give him any money unless she was quite sure he was running the station on humane lines. So they went on writing to one another, and father was getting more and more into debt, and so finally he gave in. He said she should have Irma and Leofric. I suppose he might just have sent them with Ingham the keeper to look after them, but by then my father and Miss Miall had got so at cross-purposes with one another that he thought it best to come to England himself. You see, he hadn't really managed to convince her that vivisection didn't come into his work at all——"

"And that old, mad woman, she had not managed to convince me that she had once had a canary that could discriminate between good and evil!" Virag stamped on the floor of the car.

That is to say, he thought it was the floor of the car; actually it was one of my feet. The next few minutes were swallowed up in his concern and grave apologies.

We had come to a cross-roads in the hollow of the hills; Marti had swung the car to the left. We were travelling along a lane with a low thorn hedge on either side.

I said: "Well, thanks—that fills in some of the background. And now about Miss Miall going away the morning after you arrived? . . ."

"Ah yes," said Virag, "she go away on Monday morning. She give no reason, she say she have to go."

" What did she say about coming back? "

" Soon, she say."

" And you're alone there at 2 Titmore Lane? "

" Oh no," Marti Virag replied, " there's Mrs Peach—Miss Miall's daughter."

" Her daughter? "

" Her adopted daughter. She is a very funny woman, but obliging; this is her car I'm driving."

George coughed in my ear and murmured: " Sounds to me as if the old lady's the kind that just likes adoptin' things."

" And there's Miss Teed," said Marti, " who's supposed to be Miss Miall's secretary, but she seems to do the cooking and everything else, because Miss Miall won't have any servants. . . . Oh, look! " she exclaimed excitedly. " There's Dr Glynne! "

We had just swung round a shoulder of the hill. The road was dropping steeply, with rising walls of chalk on either hand. Ahead of us in the middle of the cutting was a small car. As we came round the bend a young man climbed out of the driver's seat.

Marti exclaimed again, with warmth in her voice: " It's Dr Glynne! "

Yet as she ground on the brakes in one of those skidding stoppages that she seemed to like, it was not at the young man nor at his car that I looked, nor even at the view of far-away fields and copses, cottages and still more distant hills that opened out beyond. I looked at the house set on the hillside above us.

This solitary building, high on the steep slope of

a hill, to be reached only by a flight of steps cut into the chalk, was not the sort of house that is usually known, in this country at least, by the bleak simplicity of a number. I remembered a town in Germany where I had once noticed that the cathedral had an enamelled iron label on it: " Münsterplatz I." But that sort of thoroughness is, generally speaking, foreign to our habits; if one encounters it suddenly, one notices it, one thinks about it, one gives it significance. The fact that Rosa Miall was the sort of woman who could call that lonely dwelling 2 Titmore Lane made me feel that I had discovered something of singular interest about her.

The house was of white roughcast, two stories high, with a roof of green shingles. Its windows were large and were all, so far as I could see, framed in curtains of a rather harsh blue. The garden was in terraces; it had little growing in it but rockplants, though there were some straggly pinks bordering the steps that came down into the cutting to a white wooden gate. Awkwardly proportioned, rather as if the roughcast shell had been clapped on merely to enclose some particular pattern of rooms, the building was not specially attractive. There was no grace about it, but only a cool, business-like blankness.

The man who had just got out of the small car in the cutting waved to us, then turned to grope for something in the back of the car. He drew out a small black bag. As he stood waiting for us, his smile glanced across Virag, George and me, then settled on Marti. I could feel the excitement with which she responded to it, and there was suddenly light on her face.

She called out to him: "Dr Glynne, have you heard we have lost Irma and Leofric again?"

He replied gravely to Virag: "Yes, one of the boys who came into the surgery told me—I'm most frightfully sorry. It's a rotten thing to happen. Haven't you found them?"

Virag shook his head. "No, Dr Glynne. But now Mr Dyke is here to help me in searching, so perhaps we find them. Again, perhaps not." He introduced us.

Glynne turned his smile on me. It was the kind of smile that would undoubtedly have put heart into a patient—a bit automatic perhaps, but it lit up his tired eyes with an attractive brightness. He was about twenty-seven, with thin, sensitive, rather handsome features. He had curly brown hair and a nervous way of running his fingers through it.

He turned again to Virag. "I'm just going in to look at Mrs Peach's hand, after that I'm free for a while. Is there anything I can do? I mean, can I join a search-party or something? I wish I could help."

"You are very kind," said Virag. "We shall see. We shall consult with Mr Dyke what we are doing next. Perhaps we go and search, perhaps we merely consider the problem. I think perhaps none of us is thinking yet enough about the problem."

"I think so too, perhaps," I said.

Marti had moved up close to Dr Glynne. She

stood almost touching him as he waited beside his car, glowing at him with naïve intensity. Virag saw it and a fidgety uneasiness appeared in his glance.

Either the girl's nearness or her father's expression seemed to fluster Glynne, for he spoke in a brittle, unnatural tone: "At any rate"—and he made for the gate—"now there are such a lot of us on the job, we're bound to get your animals back safe and sound in no time."

"Just so," I said.

George said: "That's right."

"Yes, I think so too," said Virag. He was mounting the steps. "I think we get them back safe and sound."

But that was where all four of us were wrong.

When, with Virag leading the way, we had climbed the steps, gone in at the open door of the house and crossed a whitewashed hall that smelt of soap, and when Virag had thrown open the door of a long, low-ceilinged room full of oak settles, copper warming-pans, garishly blue curtains and timorous water-colours, we all saw that we were wrong.

In the middle of the room, with a terrible stain straggling across the carpet towards us, lay the distorted body of a young chimpanzee, black, hairy, bloody. It had a knife in its heart.

I WATCHED THEIR FACES.

Virag's went white and hard; something flickered and went dead in his eyes. Marti's features twitched with disgust; she gave a retching gasp, pressed both fists over her mouth and rushed from the room. Glynne stared with fascinated interest.

Yet it was from Glynne that the conventional exclamation of horror came: "Good God, how appalling!"

"It's Irma," said Virag quietly. He went forward.

I said: "Wait."

He looked at me.

"I shouldn't touch anything," I said.

"Why shall I not touch anything?"

"A crime's been committed. You'd better 'phone the police."

"No," he said.

"Yes."

"No," said Virag. "From the first they are laughing at my troubles. If Irma was a horse or a dog and this was done to her they would raise a great outcry, but Irma is a chimpanzee and they think that is funny. They say it is that I should keep my cages shut."

"You'll have to call the police," I repeated.

He stared at me without answering. Then he looked down and his gaze slid inch by inch over the black form on the ground. As if without realising what he was doing, he stirred the limp carcase with the toe of his shoe.

I suppose Irma must have been a pretty little chimpanzee in her way. She had a neat, compact body and alert, almost coquettish ears. Her black hair was parted in the middle above a low, heart-shaped forehead. She had a dainty little snub nose and her hands were small and appealing. But her eyes, wide open, had a horrible glare in them, and her lips, stretched back in a grimace, revealed the uneven, savage teeth. There was a mass of blood all over her chest and abdomen.

Glynne had edged nearer to me. He said softly: " As a matter of interest, I wonder just what kind of crime it is. You couldn't exactly call it murder, could you? "

"No," I agreed.

Yet it was as murder that I caught myself thinking of it. I have seen dead men who looked far less human in their deaths than that poor dead thing on the floor.

Glynne went on: " I wonder if it comes under some Cruelty to Animals heading, or simply the destruction of valuable property."

" Myself," I said, " I back Conspiracy."

He lifted his brows at me.

" Conspiracy to defraud," I explained. I turned to Virag. " You'll have to call the police. After all, Irma's insured, isn't she? "

Virag was staring at nothing somewhere outside the window. I had to repeat what I had said.

He gave a start and said: "Yes, yes," sounding abstracted and irritated.

"For a good deal of money?"

"Naturally. But I say I shall not call the police."

"If you want to collect the insurance, you'll have to call them. Otherwise you're liable to have difficulties with the insurance company."

He muttered to himself.

"You'll probably have difficulties with them anyhow," I told him. "This wasn't an accident."

"Very well then, I do not collect the insurance!"

"Look here," I said, "there was a motive in this madness. This was done for a purpose. I honestly don't believe you can afford to let it go at this."

He looked at me stonily.

Glynne said in a puzzled tone: "But don't you think it was done in self-defence? I know chimpanzees are pretty docile usually, but they do turn on people sometimes."

That roused Virag. He said harshly and positively: "Irma is the gentlest, most sweet-natured chimpanzee I ever know, the most trusting, the most affectionate, the most tender in all her ways—that is why I pick her for the old lady. No, as Mr Dyke say, there is a motive in this madness."

"Perhaps," I said, holding his stern, angry gaze, "you know what motive—and whose madness?"

He shook his head. Then he said abruptly: "Very well, you find out whose."

"You'll have to call the police."

"Yes, yes, I call the police, but you find out who has been killing Irma."

Glynne was saying in low, fascinated tones: "Slap into the heart—that's why there's such a phenomenal amount of blood." As I stepped forward to take a closer look at the dead animal I heard him mutter: "My God, what a mess!"

Irma had collapsed in a heap, her head tucked in between her shoulders. Her legs were bent, her hands were pressed against her breast on either side of the oozy gash into which the knife was still sticking. As Glynne had said, the amount of blood was phenomenal. It spread like a narrow, red tongue over four or five feet of carpet. Round the wound itself some flies were already buzzing.

"Not been dead long, has she?" I asked Glynne.

"A matter of minutes, I'd say."

"And bled enough for two." I stooped to examine the knife. Something odd about it struck me at once, and I murmured: "That's queer."

George was looking over my shoulder and I thought he noticed the same thing as I did.

The knife was buried up to its hilt. The hilt was a straight haft of silver about four inches long. Round the middle there was a slight projection; it was formed by a serpent in relief, twisted three times round the haft, with small, glinting rubies for eyes. Blood was splashed halfway up the hilt, covering the serpent, but above it the silver was smooth and shining.

I said to Virag: "Well, I hope this hasn't happened to your other pal, Leofric."

Virag replied: "I am expecting the worst."

"Have you seen that knife before?"

"Oh yes, I notice it in the china-cupboard there. See, the sheath is still on the shelf."

"Yes," said Glynne, "I knew I'd seen it somewhere. That's the one all right. I believe it's Chinese."

"By the way, what's that thing for?" And I pointed.

Lying near to Irma so that the tide of her life's blood had flowed over it, was a piece of bamboo about three feet long.

"Oh, that is nothing, that belongs to Irma," said Virag. "It is one of her toys—or perhaps I should call it a tool. She hook herself down pieces of banana with it."

"You see," said Glynne, and I could hear he rather liked being able to explain; his voice went fluty and a little patronising, "in a good many of the sort of experiments Dr Virag does with these chimpanzees, he's measuring their ability to think out for themselves the requirements of a given situation. For instance, if a piece of fruit is out of reach and there's a stick lying around, will the animal think of using the stick to hook down the piece of fruit?"

"And will it?"

"Oh yes, it's capable of considerably more complicated mental efforts than that."

"Then," I said, studying him, "you know a cer-

46

tain amount about this sort of work yourself? "

He gave an uncertain, humble sort of glance at Virag before he replied, then only said: " A bit."

I stood back from Irma and taking a cigarette out of a pocket, flicked it into my mouth.

" Well, Dr Virag," I said, " there are one or two things about this killing that stare one in the face. One is this—whoever did it, did it at close quarters, also he did it in the bloodiest way possible. D'you see what I mean? Some of the blood, you needn't have any doubt, got on to the killer. It got on to his hands. . . . Look at the way the stain on the hilt stops suddenly; that was where his hand came to, that's where his hand got the splashes instead of their going on to the hilt. Of course, he may have been wearing gloves, in which case his hands would have stayed clean, but he probably got some blood on to his cuffs or his wrists; it may even have splashed his waistcoat or his trousers—or her dress or her stockings——"

" You don't mean you think this was done by a woman? " Glynne broke in.

" Physically possible, isn't it? "

He made a grimace.

" The point is," I went on, " if Irma's only been dead a few minutes, the killer hasn't had much time to get rid of the blood on his hands or his clothes. Now I want to suggest, if you don't mind, that George makes a quick tour of the kitchen, the bathroom and any wash-basins there may be in the house. I suppose we ought to get permission for the search from whoever's in charge, and since Miss

Miall's away I take it that that's probably her adopted daughter. But I imagine Mrs Peach isn't at home at the present moment or she'd have heard us and come to see what's the matter. So as minutes may turn out to be precious, I suggest that Dr Virag takes responsibility for the search—in fact, it'd probably be a good thing if he went along with George, though I want George to do the searching because George is good at those things. Meanwhile, I'll get the police on the telephone."

It was George who reminded me: "There ain't no telephone, Tobe."

Glynne came to the rescue. "Shall I go and get them? Actually it might be a good idea, anyway; the local article isn't particularly good at getting a a move on, and——" He glanced at Virag doubt- fully. "You see, Dr Virag's rather upset them already; they may be inclined not to be helpful. But I'm on goodish terms with Sergeant Sawbry. Shall I go?"

I thanked him and he went.

George raised an eyebrow at Virag and Virag nodded; they went out into the hall together and I heard them start on their search for bloodstains or for any of those interesting things that George, with his singularly acute senses, is liable to pick up whenever he goes on a search.

I was left alone in the long, low drawing-room with Irma.

But I did not spend my time looking at Irma; I had seen enough of her. I wandered round the room and looked at the oak settles and pallidly refined water-colours, at the copper and brass ornaments and the ladderback chairs. Art and William Morris must at some time have made an entry into Miss Miall's life, but not, I thought, a very tempestuous entry; probably she liked this style of decoration because of the opportunities it supplied for the use of furniture-cream and metal-polish. The room had a blank, baleful cleanliness. Books collect dust—there were no books in the room. There was no electric light either, though presumably not for the same reason; there were only candlesticks with tapering orange candles in them on the mantelpiece, and two oil lamps with painted china shades. One of these lamps, I noticed, had been lit, though there was still broad daylight.

After a minute or two I went over to the window.

In terraces edged with rockroses and houseleeks the garden fell away before me. It ended in a low, stone wall. Beyond the wall came the grass with a few sheep grazing on it, and then, less than half a mile away, East Leat.

I was surprised to find the village so near. From the road it had still been hidden. But there it was, its houses and the stream that ran through the centre of the village and even the church clock beautifully visible from Miss Miall's drawing-room window. It became easier to understand why Rosa Miall had built her house up here.

There was a slight sound behind me.

While I had stood looking at the village in the valley, an astonishingly vague and beautiful blonde had drifted into the room.

She was one of those slenderly drooping blondes who look nice and cool and simple in checked gingham, which was what she was wearing. Probably she was a year or two over thirty. She had a pure, cold profile and small features, delicately white and pink. Her authentically fair and lovely hair was parted in the middle and brushed smoothly into a roll on her neck. What with that pale, shining hair and the soft colouring and the drooping grace, she had a lot more than the common share of beauty; in fact, my breath was somewhat taken away. One of her exceptionally long and narrow hands was plucking at the folds of her dress; the other hand was heavily bandaged.

Standing near the edge of the carpet she looked at a corner of the ceiling and said in a soft, blurry voice: " D'you know, I've never seen anything so revolting in my whole life? Can't someone take it away? "

I made a guess at who she was. " Not yet, Mrs Peach. It'll have to wait for the police."

" Oh, the police," she said sighingly, " how sensible. . . . All the same, why can't you take it away? I don't like looking at it—it makes me feel absolutely ill. Why don't you call Mr Ingham and ask him to take it out into the garden? That'd be better than here, don't you think? The police could look at it just as comfortably."

" I'm afraid we ought not to touch anything till the police arrive," I replied.

She experimented with a glance at Irma, but at once looked away again.

"Of course," she said accusingly, "the carpet's ruined."

"It can be cleaned," I said.

"Oh, can it? You know, I'm never practical about things like that. How marvellous." Then she looked at me suddenly as if it had only just occurred to her to be surprised at my presence. "I suppose you aren't the man from the cleaner's, are you?"

"No," I said, "I'm not."

"I thought you weren't; it was just your saying that about the carpet. . . . Besides, he's a boy usually, on a bicycle. Did you come on a bicycle?"

"No," I said.

"But you can ride one, I expect." She directed a friendly smile at the corner of the ceiling to which her gaze still clung. "There's an old one in the garage if you'd like to try it. Do just do exactly as you like while you're here. I'd offer you the car, only Miss Virag keeps borrowing it. I think the bicycle's got a puncture, but I expect it could be mended."

"I expect it could," I agreed. I am afraid I spoke with slightly nervous haste. It had just struck me that the child Miss Miall had adopted, exquisite though she was to the eye, had plainly turned out to be one of the too abundant mental-deficients of East Leat.

The lovely idiot went on sweetly, still without looking at me: "That's right—do please do exactly as you like. I don't know how to be a hostess; I hardly ever have to be one, you see, with someone

51

so very competent as Aunt Rosa about, but I always think visitors ought to do exactly as they like. And the trouble is at the moment, you see, that I haven't the faintest idea who you are or why you're here, and I'm so stupid I haven't the courage to ask you straight out. And that's partly why I'm talking such nonsense at you, because really it isn't easy to converse with a person when you haven't the faintest idea who he is—in one's own home, anyway; of course, it's different in a railway train or somewhere like that. And then if I stop talking I shall simply have to look at that thing on the floor, and really I can't bear to. And so I shall have to go on and on even if you do come to the conclusion that I'm not wholly responsible for my actions, which I can see is what you're doing."

I expect I looked uncomfortable; I may even have blushed. I cleared my throat and said: "If talking's a help, Mrs Peach, perhaps I can be of assistance to you. I can ask you a few questions, and if you like you can answer them. First, though, my name's Dyke and I'm the man whom Dr Virag got down here to look into the attempted thefts of his chimpanzees. But I've got here too late for that. Now shall I go ahead with some questions?"

"If you'd like to," she said. "You must always do just as you like here. Of course I'm dreadfully stupid and I don't expect I'll be able to tell you anything you want to know. For useful information you must always go to Miss Teed. Everyone goes to Miss Teed. Unfortunately she's out now.

I expect she's still looking for the chimpanzees. Everyone went out looking, only I didn't feel very well—this hand of mine, you see, it's poisoned and it's rather painful—so I came in and lay down, and then about half an hour ago I went out for a short walk. I came in at the front door just this moment and saw you and—this thing in here. Is that what you wanted to ask me? "

"It was," I answered drily, " exactly."

She smiled again at the ceiling.

"I'm so glad," she said. "I do like helping people when I can. You'll tell me if there's anything else at all I can do for you, won't you? But if that disgusting object really can't be moved, I think, if you don't mind, I'll go upstairs to my room again. I hope Miss Teed comes in soon, because she'll be able to be really useful, and besides, until she does I don't suppose there'll be anything to eat, because I'm so utterly hopeless with all that sort of thing. And meanwhile, do just do as you like."

She turned and vaguely, with the grace of a an absent-minded sylph, drifted out of the room.

A few minutes later George and Virag came downstairs again.

They had found nothing. Virag was looking bitter and tired and I could see that he had once more got into the mood to tell George and me to go home.

Before he had time to say anything I asked him a question: "By the way, Dr Virag, who's Mr Peach? I've heard about Mrs Peach, and I've just been having a talk with her, but I haven't heard anyone mention her husband."

Virag wrinkled his forehead. "No—no, that is true. Perhaps he is one of those husbands nobody mentions. And now perhaps you will tell me something—something I wish to know. In here some minutes ago you say something—you say as you look at Irma and the knife there: 'That's queer.' And your friend nods as if he understand you. Please, what is queer?"

I crossed the room and stood over Irma once more. I pointed. "Don't you see? That hilt's quite short; if you took hold of it, your hand would cover the whole of it. Yet there's blood up to the middle, which means that the killer's hand was gripping only the very end of the hilt. That's a funny way to grip a knife, you know—in fact, I don't think you *could* grip this one like it, unless . . ."

"Yes?" said Paul Virag.

"Unless you had uncommonly narrow hands," I answered.

*   *   *   *   *

Virag dropped on to one of the oak settles and sat with his head between his hands. I saw that my question and his own curiosity had sidetracked him only for a moment, and that he was still working himself up to the decision there and then to abandon his deal with Rosa Miall. I guessed that unless I acquiesced and allowed this unusual case to slip through my fingers, I should run into this

54

difficulty with him again and again. Paul Virag was the kind of man who finds it distasteful, even undignified, to fight for himself. Probably it was a very long time since he had had to fight for himself; until a year ago Wilfred Miall's money would have given him all the protection he needed from life's habit of arbitrary maltreatment. Probably the only technique of opposition he had ever developed was that of withdrawal, of retreat into his own thoughts, interests and indifference to his fellow creatures. Inside the defences of his own personality his own contemptuous judgment of the moral and intellectual limitations of those that assailed him would make him feel unassailable.

I said, keeping an eye on him: "We'll try that knife for finger-prints, of course."

In reply I got an impatient gesture. "What good is it? I wish we had not called in the police. I wish we do nothing. I go to America and become a professor."

"We've gone into that already," I said. "Now look here, when was the first attempt to kidnap Irma?"

"I tell you, we leave the matter." He cracked his knuckles viciously together. "I am tired, I have nothing but worry since a year. I am too tired to think in English."

"Then suppose we call your daughter to do the talking."

"No," he said quickly, "no, I do not wish it."

"Then——"

"Mr Dyke, I find you very conscientious—it is

plain to me you do not wish to take a fee without having earned it. That is admirable. And also, naturally, you do not want to go away without your fee. But please, I pay your fee, and I also apologise to you because you have been wasting your time." He gave a weary smile. "Truly, Mr Dyke, it is better if we abandon the matter."

"I think you're wrong, Dr Virag," I answered. "I think you're only storing up trouble for yourself."

"I have been storing up trouble for myself a long time, Mr Dyke."

"Do you mind telling me what you mean?"

"Yes, I mind." But he smiled again and the quality of the smile showed that he did not mean to be discourteous or hostile.

I sat down facing him, thinking it over.

"Anyway, the police have been sent for," I said, "so you can't let the thing drop. Why don't you want to get your daughter to explain things to me?"

"Because all this is bad for her. I wish I leave her in Tobago. I bring her because she has never seen Europe, but it is a mistake. I have not want to bring her, but she persuade me. She is a child, she think it very fine to see the world. Very well, I bring her. But she shall not be mixed in this, Mr Dyke. Soon I take her home and leave Europe and its kidnapping and killing and everything else to itself; I think it get on very well without us."

"But I'd sort of gathered," I said, "that unless Miss Miall came forward with the money, that home of yours in Tobago was about to cease to exist."

"Very well then, we go to America."

"Of course," I went on, "I haven't any sort of idea how much an animal like Irma's insured for. If it was a very large amount, perhaps Miss Miall's money wouldn't matter so much just for the moment."

"You are suggesting?"

"Nothing," I said. "You couldn't have had anything to do with Irma's death—either you or your daughter. You were both with me at the time Irma must have been killed."

He chewed on his lower lip. "Yes—yes, that is true."

"Now won't you tell me a few things about those earlier attempts at kidnapping?"

With his eyes on my face but with a distant look in them, Virag did some thinking. In another moment he would have spoken, only just then we heard a step in the hall. It was a slow, tired step; the door, which had been half closed, was pushed open. I heard a shuddering exclamation.

The young woman who had come in stood rigidly still just inside the doorway, staring at Irma and at the long, red tongue of blood that stretched across the carpet. All expression had been shocked out of her face.

But she recovered herself quickly, asking sharply: "How did this happen?"

"Deliberately, violently, bloodily," I replied.

"I can see that for myself, thank you."

She looked me in the face. She was about twenty-five, tall and athletically slim and straight, though at the moment her shoulders were slack with weariness. She had good features and thick brown hair and might have been attractive but for the set of her mouth, which was hard and humourless. After the first moment of horror she did her best to achieve an air of precision and certainty, but it was not much of a success; she looked too tired and desperate.

" Who did it? " she demanded.

" You can't tell us yourself, by any chance? " I asked.

" I? I've been out since six o'clock, hunting for the chimpanzees. I've only just this moment come in." She glanced at George, then back at me. " One of you must be the gentleman Dr Virag was expecting. I was starting to make a room ready for you, but then the animals disappeared—however, it won't take me long to finish. I'm Marion Teed, by the way—Miss Miall's secretary. You'll have to share a room, I'm afraid, as the house is full to capacity—unless one of you would sooner sleep in the village. But if you don't mind sharing a room we can manage. I suppose someone has gone for the police? "

I answered: " Dr Glynne went."

" I didn't know he was here," she said, looking annoyed.

" He arrived at the same time as we did. Weren't you expecting him? " I had come towards her.

" Oh, I—I knew he'd be coming some time to

attend to Mrs Peach, but I wanted to speak to him myself."

At that point I reached out and took hold of her hand. I drew it towards me and looked at it. "No doubt he'll be back. Miss Teed——"

With a startled gasp she tried to jerk her hand away.

"Miss Teed," I said, "you've been washing your hands."

She gave another wrench at her hand and I let it drop. Her muscles had gone tense, her lips had twisted and there were patches of red on her cheeks. If I had realised that she was the sort of girl who reacted like that to a touch on the hand I should have used another technique.

"But you *have* been washing your hands," I said.

She held both hands in, clenched, to her sides.

"What's that got to do with you?"

"It's just that you said you'd only this moment come in."

"Well, naturally I washed my hands when I came in."

"Ah. And where did you wash them?"

"I asked, what has it got to do with you?"

"Well, in the interests of Dr Virag, whose chimpanzee has been stabbed, I'm keeping an eye open for anyone who happens to have blood on their hands—or signs of recently having washed them."

Her eyes flickered. But she thought it over and then she said in a level tone: "I came in by the back door and I washed my hands at the kitchen sink and I dried them on the roller towel hanging on the kitchen door."

I glanced at George.

As he left the room Marion Teed said frigidly: "I'm afraid he won't find any bloodstains."

"It's a matter of routine," I said.

"I'd like you to understand," she went on, "that I'm perfectly ready to answer any questions that may help Dr Virag. I'm very shocked and distressed at what's happened. Miss Miall would be too if she were here; in fact, I think she might be rather more than . . . Well, at any rate I hope we can discover the culprit before she returns. But please ask me your questions in a straightforward way. I always prefer to deal with straightforward people. If you'd told me why you wanted to see my hands and then asked me to show them to you, I should have done so without any fuss. I never resent straightforwardness, but I can't stand trickery or——"

"Quite so," I said. "I see. I apologise."

She inclined her head slightly.

I was just wondering what a smile would look like on that face when an extraordinary noise interrupted us. It was a hooting, yelling and grunting and it came from outside the window.

At the first sound of it Virag leapt to his feet.

Something, as he did so, hurtled in at the window and landed in his arms. It was a large, black object, and it clung to him with clutching hands, nuzzling him, kissing him, squealing in an ecstasy of affection and delight. Virag's arms folded around it. He looked as Macduff might have looked if the messenger had told him that after all one of his pretty chickens had not been slaughtered.

I was advancing a few steps to look closer when a voice at the window checked me.

"Good God Almighty!" it said.

It was a deep voice, strongly American. Standing in the flower-bed under the window, looking in, was a big man, wearing a loose, rather soiled shirt and flannel trousers. The man was staring at Irma.

"Good God Almighty!" he repeated, this time almost in a whisper.

Virag turned on him with shining, excited eyes.

"How did you find him, Ingham? Where was he? It is wonderful that you find him!"

"I just found him." The man at the window went on staring at Irma and scratched his head. "Say, is there a lunatic running around loose? Why would a sane man want to do a thing like that?"

But Virag repeated: "Where have you find Leofric, Ingham?"

"I said, I just found him. He was wandering around. I guess he was scared at being alone. He fell on me the way he just did on you."

"But where—where?"

Ingham jerked a thumb. "Over in the wood."

Virag turned on me. The sagging depression was gone from his face.

"Mr Dyke, I have idea. You go with Ingham now. He take Leofric back to his cage and you go with him and ask all the questions you want. He know it all just as it has been happening and to him is no effort to think in English. Ingham——"

61

And turning back to the man at the window he poured out a flood of explanations.

Ingham nodded. Thrusting his long arms through the window he loosened Leofric's embrace of Virag, set the ape down on the ground, produced a collar and chain and fastened the collar round the furry neck. I went out and joined him in the garden. George, who had returned from the kitchen and had informed me that there were no signs of blood in the sink or on the roller towel, followed me. We set off down the terraced garden.

Evening in the Downs was incredibly still. In the very shape of those low, rounded hills there was calm. A wisp of smoke from a chimney in East Leat was hanging motionless above the roofs. I saw again the beechwood I had noticed earlier making a dark patch on the side of a hill. That was the wood, I supposed, since there was no sign of any other, where Leofric had been found.

Some distance below us, to the left, there were some low buildings. I calculated that the road, though I could not see it, must curve past them.

We had to walk slowly, adapting ourselves to Leofric's rate of progress. The chimpanzee appeared to be in excellent spirits at having found his way back to his owner; he kept up a cheerful chatter. But he seemed to feel nervous of George and me, and whenever we came near him he crowded in close to Ingham's legs.

Leofric's face was a lively and gentle one. It was full of the contemplative innocence seldom to be seen except on the faces of apes and noted mathematicians. He walked with bent knees and with his long arms dangling, the bent fingers brushing lightly against the ground.

I asked: "Is he going to be badly broken up by the death of the other one?"

"Can't say," said the keeper in his deep, slow drawl. "You noticed the old man stood in the way just now so he didn't get a glimpse of her? I guess he'll not be much upset, except at being alone—chimps never like being alone—and maybe he'll be puzzled at first. But he won't grieve, if that's what you mean. Chimps don't go in for heartbreak."

I asked if he had had long experience with them.

"I've been on this job three years," he replied.

"Then chimps haven't been your lifework?"

"Say, I'm the kind that takes any job that's going."

I gave him a glance of uncertainty; there was something about his speech that I was trying to place. But whatever it was, it eluded me. Ingham was a handsomely proportioned animal, casually muscular, with a good deal of the physical arrogance that belongs to the well-made tough. But there was something fine-drawn about his face, a curious, intelligent reserve and wariness.

I went on: "And what are your ideas about these attempted thefts and this stabbing?"

Instead of answering, the keeper said: "By the way, did the boss tell you it was my idea having someone like you along? I reckon he needs someone to take care of him. I do my best, but I don't know my way about this country. Although, as the old man says, it isn't an effort for me to think in English, I'm just a foreigner around here."

"I see," I said. "Well, have you any ideas about this lunatic slaughter?"

He answered slowly: "My only idea, for what it's worth, is that maybe it's not so lunatic as it seems. I reckon, if you think it over, you can find as many sane reasons for killing an ape as for killing a human."

"Meaning?"

He stood still and caressed the stiff, black fur of the young ape beside him.

"What would you say were the commonest reasons for the slaughter of human beings?"

"Politics, money and sex," I replied.

"I guess this is one you can leave the politics out."

"Money and sex then."

"Maybe you could put it—greed, jealousy—and hatred."

He gave a tug at Leofric's chain and we went on down the steps towards a gate in the low stone wall that encircled the garden.

"The boss'll have told you about the old woman and the will and why we're here," he said after a moment. "Not that we really know, mind you, why we're here. The old woman wanted the chimps and made that a condition of giving the boss any money, but why the heck she wanted them is one of the subjects on which I can't pass on any useful information. Maybe she doesn't really want them at all; maybe it's just that she's nuts; anyway, she cleared out the morning after we arrived. She just came to the boss and told him she'd some unexpected business to attend to and wouldn't be gone long and that he was to make himself at home, then off she went. Not that I'm missing her; she's a holy terror, one of the kind you only find sprouting in the lush, English hedgerow. It'll be no grief to me if I don't happen to see her again. All the same, so long as she's gone we aren't going to get much further with finding out what her game is, are we? "

" Mrs Peach doesn't know? "

He grinned sardonically. " I never try to find out what dames like that know."

" Well then, perhaps Miss Teed . . . ? "

" Maybe she knows, but my impression is she's not telling."

We had reached the gate in the wall. Going through it, we stepped on to dry, springy turf.

I prompted Ingham: " This greed, jealousy and hatred you were talking about? "

He looked at me sideways. " Can't you work it out for yourself? "

" I think I can work some of it out. There's money involved in the case—as I understand, a good deal of money. If Virag pulls off his deal with Miss Miall someone else is going to lose by it. It's quite conceivable that Irma may have been killed in an attempt to wreck the deal. That's greed accounted for."

Ingham nodded.

" Then jealousy," I said. " I've noticed certain

signs already that Miss Virag believes the chimps come higher in her father's affections than she does herself. Miss Virag, however, has an alibi. And that brings us to hatred."

"I shouldn't say myself that you've explored all the possibilities of jealousy when you tick Marti off the list," said Ingham. "Incidentally, you want to watch out where you are with that kid. My own opinion is that the chimps haven't been just the best possible companions for a growing girl. It's not her fault, mind you—still, you want to watch out. You're right about her though, she's jealous as hell."

"Well then," I said, "who else is suffering from jealousy?"

He was slow in replying, then negligently he said: "It's not my way to stick labels on folks, or to give them marks for their conduct. If you stay around here you'll see as much as I've seen."

Again there was something in that American voice that puzzled me. I shifted to another subject.

"I'd like to know a lot more," I said, "about these attempts at theft. I expect you know as much about them as anyone."

"Except for one person, and that's the person who did them."

"Just so," I said.

"Say, if you're thinking of connecting me with them——"

"I'm not—particularly."

"Then you must be pretty dumb," he said with a laugh, "because I'm the one who's had the opportunity; I'm the one the finger of suspicion points at."

"D'you mean," I asked, "that Virag suspects you?"

"How would I know?"

"All right, go on," I said. "What was your motive?"

"Ah," he said, with a grin, "that's where you've got me. I'm fine at thinking up motives for other people, but when it comes to working out some way I myself might have been benefited by these alleged thefts—because as far as I can see all that'll happen is I'll lose my job——"

"Alleged?" I interrupted.

He said nothing.

"Why did you say alleged thefts?" I asked. "Don't you believe in them?"

"Haven't said I don't, have I?" Standing still again, he tickled Leofric behind the ear. "I just don't know, and any ideas I've got are my own and I don't have to share them with anyone. But the way it happened was this. We were in London, putting up at some hotel where the boss had managed to persuade them to let him have the chimps along with him. They'd been in quarantine, of course, with me staying near to keep an eye on them while Virag and the kid took a look at France and Italy and some of those places. Well, the chimps were in some gardens back of this hotel, locked up in their cages. Some way or other they got away. That's all I can tell you. I found the cages open. Leofric was only a few yards off, but Irma was gone. The old man got on to the police right away, but before they showed up we'd located her; she was in a garden a couple of blocks away, mad with fear at the noise of the traffic and the strange people and all the rest of it. When the police came along all they'd do was lecture the old man on not having seen that the cages were properly locked so that dangerous animals could roam around loose on the London streets."

" Are they dangerous? "

" They can be, especially when they're older. Mostly they're friendly and anxious to make a good impression; besides, they're cowardly beasts. But they can turn nasty."

" So you think the police may have been right— I mean that it wasn't an attempt at theft at all, but just Dr Virag's carelessness, or your own."

" No," said Ingham, " the cages were locked all right."

" Had the locks been forced? "

" No."

" Just unlocked? "

" That's right."

" Then——? "

" I'm only giving you facts, not explanations."

" Well, when did the next attempt happen? "

" Last Tuesday," he replied.

" When you'd been here how long? "

" Two days."

" And how did it happen? "

" Same way as the first time. I found the cages —they'd got padlocks on 'em by then as well as locks and bolts—simply standing open. Leofric as before hadn't got far; he's less skittish than Irma, he likes to stay home. But it took us hours to find Irma—and then it wasn't us that found her. Some folks came up from the village saying she was down there scaring the life out of some old woman's chickens. The village was in a state of uproar; people were afraid to touch her, and there she was, prodding at the hens through the wire and grinning all over her face when they dashed around cackling. There was a delegation to Miss Miall from the village that evening; I think what they said was that if she let it happen again they'd have the law on her."

" Almost a state of revolution, considering the sort of position Miss Miall appears to occupy in East Leat."

He answered dourly: " All the same, it made things look serious for us when this evening it happened again."

" Was it just the same as before? "

" Just the same."

" But I should have thought," I said, " that after those two attempts you'd have been keeping a pretty close eye on the chimps."

" Say," he exploded, " I've been sleeping down there, I've been eating down there—and if that kid Marti hadn't let me down over the cigarettes——"

" Ah, you were fetching cigarettes when it happened? "

He nodded grimly. " As I said, that kid Marti had promised to bring me some cigarettes when she brought my lunch along. She didn't; she said she forgot. She said she'd bring me some later. I reckon she forgot again. I hung out till about half-past five, then I went to get them myself. I knew I'd not be gone more than fifteen minutes. Fifteen minutes! " He cursed. "When I came back the chimps were gone."

George made his first contribution to the conversation. "You don't think it's just that they're bein' let out by someone who don't like the idea of keepin' animals in captivity? I had a girl once who wouldn't even go walkin' out in Regent's Park in case she saw the poor animals in their cages."

Neither Ingham nor I found it necessary to reply to this suggestion.

We walked on down the steep slope towards the buildings by the road.

One of these was a garage. The other was a store-house of some kind—long, narrow and rather dark. Its door was open and in the shadows I could see as we approached the shapes of garden tools and odd pieces of furniture, a broken rocking-horse and other lumber.

Ingham, ushering Leofric in ahead of him, looked round and said: "Mind you, there's no need for anyone to waste time slaughtering these beasts, because they'll be dead anyhow in a few weeks. It takes expert knowledge to keep them alive in this climate—and just look at the lousy hole the old woman's provided for them. No air, no light—it's scarcely fit for rabbits. Say——" He broke off, staring.

At the far end of the long, narrow storehouse, in front of some contraptions of wood and iron, a figure was standing. I remember that for a moment, and with a curious sense of shock, I thought that it was Rosa Miall.

It was the shadows that let me make this mistake. Before my eyes had got to work properly I had jumped to the conclusion that the huge figure in black with its back to us, wearing a long skirt that almost touched the floor, was that of an old woman —a huge, thick, lumpy old woman. At the same time I had a sudden feeling that there was something sinister and obscene there in the shadows.

But it was not only because of the unnatural size of what I took to be an old woman that I had that feeling of revulsion; it was also because of what the figure was doing. Even when I had realised that it was a man I was looking at, a man in the long, black habit of a priest, the sense of shock remained. For he was shaking his fist. Trembling in a desperate agony of rage, he stood there shaking his fist at the empty cages.

I felt Ingham's breath on my cheek as he put his lips close to my ear: " Say, when we were going over the reasons for killing an ape, we forgot to account for hatred, didn't we? "

*　　*　　*　　*　　*

The man turned.
He was about sixty, massive and paunchy, with a round, yellow moon of a face. It was a face which might simply have been a sack of skin stuffed full of marbles that had pushed it out into little, lumpy, hard features. The eyes were like yellow glass

marbles, veined with red. I assumed then, not knowing much about details of clerical dress, that the long, black habit meant he was a Roman Catholic; actually he was high-church Anglican. He stood gazing at us with his rage still stiffening him and his fist still raised. Leofric, flinging his arms round Ingham's legs for protection, let out shrill squeals of suspicion.

The man coughed slightly. He came a few steps towards us, walking with heavy, swinging strides.

" Dr Virag? " he said to Ingham.

Ingham looked him up and down. " What the hell are you doing here? "

" I'm sorry if I'm intruding." The voice was a cultured one, but unpleasantly fruity and the words blundered out too hurriedly after one another. " I knew of Miss Miall's interesting acquisition and as I was on my way up to the house I thought I'd look in. The door was open, you see, and Miss Miall's quite used to my informal ways. It's really most interesting. Most—most."

" That's right," said Ingham, " empty cages *are* interesting."

The yellow eyes gleamed. " I meant the monkeys."

" Apes."

" Most interesting—though bizarre, and—well, of course, in East Leat we're all used to our surprising but invaluable Rosa Miall. I'm just on my way up to the house to discuss certain matters with her now. So if you'll excuse me——"

" Miss Miall's away."

He frowned. "Oh, is she, is she indeed?" His jaws worked against one another as if he were chewing gum. "Well, Dr Virag——"

"I'm not Dr Virag," said Ingham. "I'm the keeper."

"Ah. And I suppose you've just been taking the —the apes for a little walk. How interesting."

"I've just been taking one of them for a walk. The other's dead."

The man in black started. Curious, deep wrinkles appeared suddenly between his nose and his mouth. He looked surprised, then concerned. But the first thing I saw on his face before either the surprise or concern was some emotion far fiercer than either.

"Dear me, *dead*?" The gum-chewing motion of his jaws began again.

"You heard me," said Ingham.

It struck me all at once that those deep wrinkles on the clergyman's face meant that he was trying not to smile.

He coughed again. "I'm so sorry to hear it—so very sorry. I suppose after its unfortunate escapade last Tuesday you decided it was dangerous and it had to be shot. Poor thing. And poor, dear Miss Miall—such a disappointment for her. I—er—know how much the acquisition of these animals meant to her."

I moved forward a little. "Shot, did you say?"

The clergyman gazed at me over Ingham's shoulder. "Well, er, wasn't it?"

"Why shouldn't it have died a natural death?" I asked.

" Dear me, I'm afraid I just leapt to the conclusion that——"

" Don't you know," I said severely, " that it takes expert knowledge to keep chimpanzees alive in this climate? "

He nodded his head. The wrinkles had gone; the skin of his face sagged flabbily over the marbles once more. " Quite so, quite so. But after all, the animals have only just arrived. However, some sickness, I suppose, contracted on the journey . . ."

" As a matter of fact," I said, " she was stabbed."

He seemed to rear up at that. *" Stabbed? "*

" In the heart," I said. " Messy business. Blood all over Miss Miall's best carpet."

With pursed lips, looking sick and disgusted, the man in black turned away.

Ingham, still sour and suspicious, said pointedly : " Mr Dyke here is kind of on the look-out for whoever did it."

" And you're not Dr Virag, you say? " said the other, looking at him again.

" No, my name's Ingham—Christopher Ingham."

" Thank you. Let me introduce myself too— Alexander Teed. I'm the vicar of East Leat. I expect you've met my niece, Marion. She's Miss Miall's secretary. D'you know, I—I feel I've met you before, Mr Ingham."

Ingham raised his eyebrows.

" Yes, I really feel sure . . ." said the vicar.

Ingham, beginning to push Leofric forward, urging him towards the cages, asked indifferently, " You've been to the States—or the West Indies maybe? "

"Never. In fact, I've never been out of England."

"Then I reckon we've never met."

"This is your first visit here?"

"Yes."

Furrows appeared on the smooth bank of yellow skin that composed the vicar's forehead. "It's really your first visit? Forgive my curiosity, because I feel sure . . . However, I can't place where . . . I've scarcely been out of East Leat for ten years. Before that I was in the East End of London. I landed in East Leat, alas, because of my health and for no other reason. You're quite sure you've never been to East Leat, or Ashingham, or——"

"No, nor in any of your Thames-side health resorts either."

"Come to think of it, one day in Ashingham——"

Ingham rounded on him. "What *is* this? I told you, I've never been in this darned country before. Can you understand that, or would you like me to spell it over?"

Teed laughed urbanely. "Oh, it's a mistake on my part, of course. But resemblances can be very haunting, can't they? And they occur so often, don't you think? Or perhaps it's only that I've rather a knack of noticing them. I often say to myself that the good God created us from a very few patterns." He laughed again, a coy-sounding little professional titter.

"Having copied us in the first place," I put in, "from an earlier model." I pointed at Leofric.

But the vicar went prim and supercilious at that; I

suppose he had professional objections to the idea of evolution. His next remark bore this out.

"And you say," he said rather anxiously, "that the other monkey was stabbed—through the heart? Horrible! Horrible and—blasphemous! As if it were human. . . ."

"By the way," I said, "how long were you in here, Mr Teed, before we found you?"

My abrupt question produced a silence.

Suddenly there was a muddled, apprehensive look in the vicar's eyes. Then he leapt about two feet into the air.

As he came to earth again I heard Ingham cursing at Leofric.

The young chimpanzee had picked up a length of bamboo that had been on the floor of the cage. He had waited until Teed had moved into a suitable position, then, pushing the bamboo through the bars of the cage, had jabbed at the vicar fiercely from behind. Hence Mr Teed's surprising levitation.

Ingham slapped Leofric and said: "Sorry, Mr Teed. Great sense of humour, chimps have. You want to watch out."

"So I perceive." Smiling thinly, Teed induced himself by strong self-discipline to take it as a joke. "Your job must be most amusing, Mr Ingham, most amusing."

"Just one big laugh after the other," Ingham agreed.

"Now, Mr Dyke"—Teed turned again to me—"you've just asked me a question. You want to know how long I was in here before you came in?

You consider your question, I assume, in some way relevant to the shocking event you've just told me about—that stabbing, I mean. Very well, I don't in the least mind telling you. I should have felt it was more fitting perhaps if it had been a member of the police force who had asked me the question, but all the same, out of respect for our dear Rosa Miall, I will, if you desire it, lay bare my whole life to you, every detail of my—er—uprising and down-sitting! "

" Thanks," I said.

" Now, let me see. . . ." He looked up thoughtfully at the murky ceiling. " How long was I in here? About two minutes, I'd say. Or perhaps less. I was lost in thought and I can't really remember. I'd walked up the hill from the village and had sat down on the grass out there by the roadside, admiring the view and smoking a cigarette. My health, you see—I can't manage these hills too well—I generally rest there for a bit when I come up to see Miss Miall. Anyway, that's beside the point. What you want to know is, just how long was I in this building? Well, at a guess, two minutes. I hope the information is of use to you."

I was not, as a matter of fact, particularly concerned with the precise amount of time the vicar had spent in this building. Much more I should have liked to know what he had been doing with himself a little earlier. I glanced at George, who got my meaning and slipped out quietly into the road to check up on the cigarette the vicar said he had smoked.

Teed was putting a large, shovel hat on his head.

"Well, gentlemen," he said, "I think, even if Miss Miall is away, I'll now continue on my way up to the house. I want a word with my niece Marion. A remarkable girl, you know—so spontaneously good. But it troubles me that she works so hard; I'm often afraid her health will suffer for it. Lately she hasn't been looking at all well. I frequently intend to expostulate about it with our dear Rosa Miall. That amazing woman, she means so well, but she doesn't realise that we don't all possess her astounding energy. Having ruined my own health by overwork—though, of course, I don't regret it—I look on with great concern when I see signs of the same thing happening to somebody else. Besides, I fear Marion's surrounded by influences which ... However, perhaps I shall see you up at the house later? But in case I don't—good evening."

In the silence that followed the vicar's exit I heard Ingham turn the key of the cage.

He said: "There are things going on here I don't like, and folk I don't much take to. I'll be glad when we're back in Tobago."

"Odd he was so sure he'd seen you before," I observed.

"Is that so?"

"Well, isn't it?"

"He's nuts," said Ingham.

I frowned, again trying to make up my mind what it was about his voice that worried me. He had just thrust one hand through the bars of the cage and was fondling Leofric's head when suddenly I remembered something.

" By the way," I said, " would you let me take a look at your hands? "

He hesitated, then he held them out.

They were big hands, strong, with brown, work-roughened skin. Their shape was fine, wide in the palm, with long, square-tipped fingers. They were rather dirty, with tobacco-stains on the first and second fingers and with black under the nails and round the jagged cuticle. Certainly he had not washed them recently. But there was no blood on them.

" Thanks," I said.

As, rather self-consciously, Ingham thrust his hands into his pockets, George appeared in the doorway.

" Say, Tobe, that bloke was correct about his habit of down-sittin' out there," he said. " There's a regular heap of cigarette-stubs collected in the ditch, and three of them are brand-new. So I reckon he was sittin' there for a bit this evenin', like he said. Maybe he was there for as long as half an hour."

I nodded, visualising again that huge, black blot of a man, as I had first seen him, standing in the shadows shaking his fist at the empty cages.

It was then that George, with that irritating habit he has of putting his finger straight on to the thing that has been worrying me—sometimes for days—turned and remarked casually to Ingham: " Say, Mr Ingham, you aren't an American, are you? "

I saw Ingham's eyes go hard.

But that was what it was; I knew George was right. The man's voice, his accent, his phraseology. . . .

He said: " So I'm not an American? "

He said it quietly, looking George in the face.

"No, Mr Ingham," said George in his gentle, reasonable way, " you're as English as I am."

" I'm an American," said Ingham.

"No," I joined in. " Perhaps you do it well enough to take in Virag, whose own knowledge of English isn't impressive—and for all I know, you may be an American citizen. But you didn't suck up that accent with your mother's milk."

The muscles of Ingham's shoulders tightened. I was watching his eyes, and at what I saw in them I went taut, waiting for him.

But, turning away, he used his fist to give Leofric a playful punch through the bars.

" Have it your own way," he said with a negligent laugh. " It's nothing to me what you think. I'm an American."

—— III ——

THE FIRST PERSON we saw when George and I got back to the house was Marion Teed. She heard us as we came in at the front door, and emerging from the kitchen wearing a white overall, told us that the police had arrived and that they were at present with Dr Virag in the sitting-room.

"I think Sergeant Sawbry will want to speak to you presently, Mr Dyke," she said, "but I can take you up to your room now if you like. I'm afraid there won't be a meal of any sort ready for about half an hour, and even then you'll just have to put up with what there is; I don't feel like tackling a real job of cooking at the moment. Where did you leave your baggage?"

We had left the suitcases in the car. As George went to fetch them I looked at the girl's tired face and at the limp way she immediately propped herself against the banisters to wait.

I asked: "Is nobody helping you?"

"Miss Virag's helping," she replied.

"I'm quite good at working a tin-opener," I said, "and George is good at nearly everything."

"Thanks very much," she answered, "but it's my job; I'm used to it."

"D'you mean you do everything about the house?"

81

Listlessly, as if she were too weary to talk, she said: "When Miss Miall's at home she does the cooking."

"But——"

"Are you surprised"—she looked at me with amusement in her cold yet strangely desperate eyes —"that someone as rich as Miss Miall should do her own cooking and expect her own secretary-companion to do the housework?"

"Yes," I said, "I'm definitely surprised. It isn't usual."

"There are a good many things about Miss Miall you won't find usual."

"So I understand."

She frowned at my tone, and quickly, defensively, began to explain: "You see, until Miss Miall was about forty she'd very little money. It was the same with her brother, you know. They both inherited their money from an uncle, but not until they were middle-aged. Miss Miall had been living up here for about fifteen years already, managing on two hundred a year, and she was used to it and liked it. She'd really got everything she wanted; she's always cared more about doing things than possessing things, and——"

"Doing certain sorts of things can be pretty expensive," I said. "Travelling, for instance."

"Oh, she never wanted to travel or to do anything for mere pleasure. She always wanted to reform things, improve things, help people——"

"And boss 'em about? But you can do even that a good deal better if you've lots of money."

" Ye-es," said the girl. " But I think Miss Miall was pretty good at it even before she had any money —that's where she's different from many people. Anyway, when she suddenly inherited all that money she made only one alteration in her way of living—she adopted a baby. Apart from that, she's often told me, she didn't change anything at all; she went on just as if her income were still two hundred a year. It was only two years ago that she made up her mind to employ a companion-secretary, and that was only because she'd been very ill and couldn't cope with the house and the garden and all her committees and correspondence and obligations by herself."

" Why didn't she employ a cook, a gardener and a secretary, reduce unemployment and not overwork any of them? "

" Surely," she said, " it's one of the advantages of being rich that one can live as one wants to."

" And make others live as one wants them to? "

" But she doesn't," said the girl; " she's most considerate."

" You don't look as if she were."

She brushed a hand across her forehead. " Really, it isn't Miss Miall's fault. She *is* very thoughtful and considerate—though some people don't realise it. You see, if she were here now she'd be doing lots of the work herself; it's the fact that she's away, and that there are all these extra people, and that I'm upset about——" Suddenly, sharply, she checked herself.

" That you're upset and worried about something quite different? "

She turned away. Moving to the open doorway through which George was to be seen bringing the two suitcases up the steep garden steps, she stood with her back to me.

After an instant she turned her head.

" I'll be delighted to answer any questions you want to ask me about the chimpanzees, Mr Dyke."

I left it at that. As George came in at the door the girl jerked herself into briskness, crossed to the foot of the stairs, and with a slight movement of her head indicated that we were to follow her.

The room to which she took us was a small room with a divan in it and a camp-bed. She apologised for the camp-bed. The room was as scrubbed and polished as all the others in the house, with the usual harsh blue curtains. There was a couple of handwoven rugs on the floor, and there were some Japanese prints on the walls. At one end of the room there was a french window which opened on to what I took to be a balcony. It was not a balcony, however; it was a lawn; the rooms on the upper floor at the back of the house opened straight on to the garden; the hillside sloped so steeply that the house had been built right into it.

I pushed the glass doors open and looked out.

The ground had been levelled back for a few yards. Enclosed by a curved precipice of chalk was a small lawn with a bright border of flowers. There was a wooden bench against the house. The top of the hill, edging a sky turning pale and faint with the dusk, was not far above us.

The girl told us that she would let us know as soon as Sergeant Sawbry wanted us.

As she went out I dropped on to the divan and stretched out my legs.

" You know, George," I said, " I could bear to know a whole lot more than I do about Rosa Miall."

For that, all through this case, was what I kept coming back to.

George opened a suitcase and started to unpack.

" Rosa Miall," I went on thoughtfully, " the mystery woman of East Leat. . . . Aren't you rather curious about her yourself, George? "

" Curious ain't all I am," said George.

I lay back with my hands under my head. " A woman who has the idea of keeping chimpanzees must have something interesting about her. I'm wondering very much indeed what she's meaning to do with them. And I'm wondering almost as much what she's up to now. It's certainly rather odd the way she walked out on her guests. Even supposing she didn't like the look of them when they turned up, it's contrary to the grand old tradition of British hospitality. What d'you think, George? "

George was unpacking a toothbrush and toothpaste at the wash-basin. " I think," he said, " you could make a fair guess that her goin' off like that had got somethin' to do with the chimps."

" Of course it's got something to do with the chimps. For one thing, it's obvious she's made no serious preparations for keeping them here, which, in the efficient sort of individual she appears to be, is strange." I sat up again. "George, what's the name you'd apply to this crime?"

"Well, plain, bloody murder's good enough for me—I liked the look of that monkey."

"No, George," I said, "it's conspiracy—conspiracy to defraud. There's someone who doesn't want Dr Virag to get the money for his experimental station."

"Not forgettin'," said George, "that besides greed there's jealousy and hatred. . . ."

"Certainly I'm not forgetting. But at the moment I'm backing the financial motive—at least, I'm giving it my attention. D'you know what I've been wondering ever since I saw that dead animal downstairs? It's what Miss Miall would do with her money if she didn't give it to Dr Virag. Marion Teed's just told me that last time Miss Miall inherited a lot of money she never made any use of it, but went on living precisely as she'd done before. I don't see why a second fortune should make her change her habits. I should think it's quite likely that there's someone about who thinks they've a good chance of getting their hands on that money if only its present trend in the direction of Dr Virag can be changed. Then I'm wondering too if Miss Miall's made a will, and if so, how she's made it. It seems she had a serious illness two years ago, and besides, she must be fairly old. There may be someone about who's thinking of the future, the probably not-so-distant future. Then I'm wondering——"

"I'll tell you what I'm wonderin', Tobe." George

was taking a pair of bedroom slippers out of the suitcase. "I'll tell you what I been wonderin' ever since we come into that room downstairs and seen that monkey lyin' in that pool of blood. I'm wonderin', why did they have to move the monkey?"

I looked at him.

"Yes, Tobe," he said, standing there with a slipper in each hand, "they moved her right the minute after they'd killed her. Anyone could see that. The pool of blood was sort of like a tongue, wasn't it?—a long, narrow tongue. Why, I reckon it was as long as four feet or maybe five——"

"Of course, of course!"

I jumped to my feet.

It is extraordinary how often George manages to pick on details that make my mind start working with a beautiful, swift lucidity.

I started walking up and down the room. At each three strides I had to turn, but with my eyes half-closed I shut out most of the small, confined room with its blue curtains and with George standing there with the hideously checked felt slippers in his hands.

"Of course that's it," I said. "Irma was moved. Blood won't flow four or five feet along a horizontal surface, and a carpet at that, that's going to suck up a good deal. Of course she was moved. She was stabbed and the blood gushed out on to the carpet, then she was dragged back a couple of feet from where she'd fallen, and the blood went on flowing until it linked up with the first pool of blood."

87

" That's right, Tobe—but why? Why did they have to move her? "

" Presumably because they were trying to take her away, trying to get her out of the house. But they heard the noise of us arriving in the car and did a bolt——"

" Out of the window? "

" Yes, yes, out of the window! There was no one in the house when we came in, was there? But if the killer had come out by the front door we'd have seen him."

" There's the back door—and he might have dashed upstairs and popped out through here."

" I tell you, it's much more likely he got out by the window. Even to dash across the hall would have been a risk; the front door was standing open and we might have seen in. No, George, the killer got out by the window, *and*——" I turned on him and grabbed him by the shoulder. " *And left foot-prints in the flower-bed outside !* "

" Which Mr Christopher Ingham come and stood in a few minutes later," said George unenthusiastically.

" Damn ! " I said.

I dropped back on to the divan and chewed at my lips.

" Damn," I said again, " damn that phoney American ! "

George kicked the empty suitcase shut and pushed it under the camp-bed. He took a comb out of his pocket and began to comb his hair. I sat on the edge of the divan, holding my head in my hands, staring down at the red and green stripes of the handwoven rug under my feet. It was a reasonably hideous rug, but my sight was glazed in a wild chase of thought.

George said: "Anyway, that's all guessin'—we don't know for certain why they moved the monkey, and we didn't ought to start thinkin' we did."

"There's only one thing we know for certain," I said, "and that's that neither Virag nor Marti Virag could have done it. They were both with us. And Glynne arrived with us. But Mrs Peach simply says she was out for a walk, and Ingham and Marion Teed both say that they were out looking for the chimps, apparently not together. Then there's the vicar, who could easily have manufactured his cigarette-stub alibi. So unless any of them can produce someone who saw them, they're all equally suspect. And of them all, Mrs Peach, Miss Miall's adopted daughter, who will probably inherit most of Miss Miall's fortune, and has probably the most easy access now to her money—of them all, Mrs Peach is the one in whom I'm most definitely interested. I'd very much like to know a great deal more about Mrs Peach."

"Ain't you forgettin'," said George, "that the first time the beasts got loose was in London?"

"No," I replied, "I'm not forgetting it. I'm not forgetting either that Mrs Peach has got a husband somewhere—so why not in London?"

There was a tap at the door. It was Marion Teed, who had come to tell us that we were wanted by Sergeant Sawbry.

The interview that followed was a barren one. Sergeant Sawbry's manner was abrupt; he edged his questions with sarcasm. He seemed to feel that in the manner of Irma's death there was something aimed personally at him, some gibe, some deliberate mockery. I daresay he had often had daydreams about what he would do if only one of the inhabitants of East Leat would one day have the enterprise to stick a knife into another inhabitant of East Leat; now his dream had been travestied; Fate had presented him with an offensive parody of his ambition. Resentful and on the defensive about it, he refused to take it seriously as a crime. I think Virag had been right when he suggested that if Irma had been a horse or a dog Sawbry would have been ready to race hot-footed on the trail of the perverted scoundrel who had done her to death; but a chimpanzee was something outlandish, something that ought to have no existence except in a circus. In that black, bloody form on the carpet the sergeant refused to recognise anything but a shocking mixture of the indecent and the ridiculous.

Besides, as I discovered later, it was Sawbry's sister-in-law's aunt's chickens that Irma had frightened on her trip to the village.

Ponderously amused about my presence, he inquired with leaden irony if I had discovered any useful clues. By the time he had finished with me I had made up my mind that unless some other police-officers put in an appearance and showed that they were ready to treat Dr Virag's loss with respect, I should have to go to Ashingham and appeal to someone there to take the case over.

While Sawbry was questioning me I strolled across to the window. I leant out and looked at the flower-bed. Ingham's footprints were there in the softly raked soil—but only Ingham's, which were large enough and deep enough to have obliterated any that might have been there before them. It was not at all helpful.

*   *   *   *   *

When Sawbry had finished with me I found my way to the dining-room.

In a silent group at one end of the room I found the two Virags, Dr Glynne and the vicar. The table was laid. Looking round, I saw no signs of a drink, which was more or less as I had expected; all the same, it depressed me. I noticed also that no one was smoking and that there were no ashtrays in the room. This depressed me still more. My faculties are never at their best when the rule is no drinking, no smoking.

While we waited I could see that the vicar was nearly desperate for a cigarette. The man could not keep his hands still; they jerked and twisted and fought a battle of scratching and pulling with the arms of his chair. It was upsetting to watch them. I noticed that it was getting on Glynne's nerves as well as on mine, for every now and then his mouth pulled over to one side and he let his breath out slowly as if he had just succeeded in stifling a furious exclamation.

The meal was delayed because it was Marion Teed who was being questioned.

I was wondering how I could find out more about Mrs Peach's position in the household. Was she dependent on Miss Miall or on the husband that nobody mentioned? Was she in fact the person who would lose if Miss Miall were to proceed with the endowment of Dr Virag's experimental station? What sort of person was she? What went on in her mind behind that sweet-faced idiocy? As I stood watching the vicar's fidgeting and the doctor's irritation, these questions kept on churning in my brain. Also my thoughts kept coming back curiously to Mr Peach. Who was he? What was he? Where was he? Most important of all, where had he been last Saturday, the day on which the first attempt at theft had been made?

Presently Mrs Peach drifted into the dining-room and sat down at one end of the table. She fixed her dreamy gaze on one corner of the ceiling. Glynne sat down beside her and started talking to her in low tones. I did not catch much of the conversation. Glynne seemed to be talking about her bandaged hand and she to be telling him not to bother about it. Glynne's fingers went clawing nervously through his hair. At the other end of the room Marti Virag stirred suddenly, her chair scraping sharply on the polished floor. She was staring at the two of them with big, anxious, jealous eyes, digging her teeth into her lip.

I felt rather sorry for her. As Glynne leant towards the slim, blonde woman at his side, his gaze was hard with a hungry concentration. There was no chance of doubting the state of his emotions, and I doubt if he knew that Marti Virag existed.

Presently Marion Teed came in, carrying a bowl of salad and a dish of cold meat. Putting them down on the table she said dully: "The police have gone and they've taken Irma." Dropping into a chair at the table, she put her head on her hands. We took our places and Mrs Peach started serving the cold meat.

Plates were handed past Marion, but she did not lift her head until a plate was put down before her. Then she said, glancing up for a moment: "Thanks —I don't want anything."

Mrs Peach blinked at her. "Not want anything? Why, good gracious——"

Quickly, irritatedly, Marion repeated: "Thanks —I said, I don't want anything."

"But you *must* have something," said Mrs Peach, gesturing vaguely with the fork she held. "Mustn't she, Kenneth?"

"Of course," said Glynne.

"Please give me some salad," said Marion, "and I'll take this plate down to Mr. Ingham. He won't leave Leofric."

"Please," said Virag, "Marti shall take the plate to Ingham. You are tired, Miss Teed; you must sit down and eat."

"I'll take it," said George.

"I'll go, I'll go!" said Marion, with the fierce irritation of the overwrought. "I really couldn't eat anything if I tried. Please give me some salad and——"

"But whatever's the matter, Marion?" asked Glynne.

"Nothing, nothing—I'm just not hungry."

"My dear girl, don't be absurd," he said.

"You didn't have any tea," said Mrs Peach, still waving the fork.

"I tell you, I don't want anything!" Marion's voice jerked on to a higher note and she pushed her chair back. She looked round at us all. The state of tension she was in was certainly strange. She met the uneasy glances of the people at the table with an angry, defensive stare. They all looked very uneasy, very disturbed. Her hysterical tone seemed to be something with which they were not familiar.

"Marion, my dear," said the vicar, thrusting his big, yellow face towards her, "you're letting the distressing affair of the chimpanzee get on your nerves—and of course you've been doing too much, scouring the countryside looking for the animals, besides working away in the house. But if you'll just sit down quietly and have a good meal you'll feel ever so much better."

"Of course you will," said Mrs Peach. "Why, you must be ravenous. You didn't have any tea and I remember you ate scarcely anything at lunch. I believe you've just got so tired you think you aren't hungry—it happens like that, you know. What you've got to do is sit down and simply make yourself eat, then you won't feel so upset or so tired either."

"That's it," said Glynne, "it's just that you're tired."

It struck me they were all very anxious to convince her that she was tired—or perhaps, it suddenly occurred to me, it was all aimed at me. At all events, they seemed to be in a great hurry to get the fact established that Marion Teed was simply tired, nothing but tired, that there was no other reason for the hysteria that rasped in her tone.

George managed to get hold of the plate of cold beef and carried it off to Ingham.

Virag leant forward. In his sombre, courteous way he said: "Miss Teed, if you permit, I make a recommendation. A little brandy or whisky. It revive you and then you have appetite."

"No, thank you," she said coldly.

A little titter came from the huge bulk of the vicar.

"Brandy, whisky! My dear Dr Virag, not a drop of either of those two excellent beverages is ever to be found in this house. Miss Miall believes in the strictest abstinence. Plainly you had not much chance to get acquainted with her before she was called away on her—er—business. You couldn't have conversed with her for long without discovering that abhorrence of alcohol is, well, almost the basis of her social philosophy."

"Oh, that's absolutely true, Dr Virag," said Mrs Peach. "It may seem funny to you, but I think Aunt Rosa's really wonderful—so full of principles and everything. I wish I was more like her."

"Myself," the vicar continued, attacking his cold beef, "I always feel that the trouble is that Miss Miall isn't a religious woman. If she were, I'm sure I could convince her that the good God never placed

95

any prohibition on our enjoyment of His blessings. I could quote chapter and verse. But as she's what you might call a good, old-fashioned, nineteenth-century agnostic, with all the humanitarianism, the puritanism and impiety of her kind——"

"Uncle Alex," Marion Teed cut in, her voice controlled again but still too tense, "I don't think you should attack Miss Miall when she isn't here."

"I'm not attacking her, my dear," said the vicar. "I was merely explaining——"

"You are," she said uncompromisingly.

"Ah well," he replied, with another giggle, "I shouldn't have the courage to do it if she were here —you know that."

"Yes," she said, "I do know it."

"You also know," he said, "that no one respects her more than I do. I respect her singleness of purpose, her disinterestedness, her obstinacy, her disregard of conventional methods and her passionate desire to improve mankind. From the bottom of my heart I disagree with almost everything she does, but I have the deepest respect for the courage and energy with which she does it."

"You only say that, you don't mean it. If you were sincere you'd admit you detested her." The girl's hurt, humourless glance swept round the table. "You all detest her—and you're all frightened of her."

I saw Glynne and Mrs Peach exchange glances. When Glynne looked back at Marion he had a worried, considering look in his eye. But I noticed that no one contradicted her.

I said: "I haven't met Miss Miall, and the more I hear of her the more I regret it. Without meeting her it seems to be pretty difficult to understand her, and without understanding her I don't think I've much chance of understanding this case. I want to understand it, however; I want to solve Dr Virag's problem."

"We all want you to solve it," sighed Mrs Peach, her gaze slipping languorously up to the corner of the ceiling.

"Good," I said. "Then, if you don't mind, I'd like to ask a question. It's a good opportunity since we're all here and I don't happen to know who the person is that can answer me."

"Perhaps none of us can answer you," said Marti Virag in a low voice, looking down at her plate. "Or perhaps—no one will."

"And we aren't all here, you know," said Mrs Peach, crumbling bread beside her plate. "Mr Ingham isn't here."

"I doubt if he's the person I want," I said. "This is a question for the home team. I'll have others for Ingham later. Quite simply I want to know, why did Miss Miall want the chimpanzees?"

The answer to my question was silence. I had half expected it would be. Then, after a moment, there was a suddenly increased interest in mustard and salad-dressing; people started reaching for things, passing things to one another, making fidgety movements.

Marti Virag fixed dark eyes on my face. "What did I tell you?"

Mrs Peach burst out plaintively: "But I can't tell anyone about anything because I simply don't know anything—I never do."

"I'm afraid I can't help you, Mr Dyke," said Glynne.

"Nor I," said Virag grimly. "I cannot think why an old lady, even one who is known as an eccentric, should want two chimpanzees."

I looked at Marion Teed.

"I know nothing about it," she said.

Leaning back in his chair, the vicar gave his wheezily sardonic giggle. "The mystery is complete. Nobody knows." He pulled down the corners of his mouth in a mocking grimace. "I fear, Mr Dyke, you'll believe that somebody here isn't telling the truth, and I think I agree with you. I feel quite certain that others besides myself know why Miss Miall wants the chimpanzees."

His niece turned on him. "*Besides yourself?*"

"Oh yes," he said, smiling. "I know all about it."

Marion Teed went a little slack in her chair. Then she shrugged her shoulders. "Oh well, if you know . . ."

Her uncle put his elbows on the table and folded his hands under his chin. He had a trick of taking up rather feminine attitudes which his great, ponderous size helped to make singularly repellent. "Yes indeed," he said, "I know everything."

"Then," said Virag, "perhaps you are explaining to Mr Dyke what he wish to know?"

"Yes," said Teed, "yes, I shall be most pleased to do so. Knowledge of this sort"—he cleared his

98

throat and leered ironically—"is a heavy responsibility. One is glad to share it. May I say, Mr Dyke, that I think you were right when you said that in order to understand this fantastic case, you would have to understand Miss Miall. Unfortunately, I haven't the slightest belief that you'll succeed in doing so. I have never done so myself. I have never been able to understand characters in which goodness takes such unaccountable forms, becoming indistinguishable, to my poor vision, from pride and perversity. However, I ought not to judge your powers of understanding by my own. I must make it clear too that I have no doubt that at the moment Miss Miall's actions are being dictated purely by her conscience and that only her relentless passion for promoting the good of others is responsible for her latest, most singular crusade."

Marion muttered bitterly: "You're in her house —you've got no right to laugh at her."

"Who's laughing at her?" he inquired blandly. "You see, Mr Dyke, Miss Miall has given herself, given her whole life, to the good of East Leat. Perhaps you've heard of her crusade to bring motorbuses out here. Not everyone—myself included— considers this an advantage. But it was Miss Miall's belief that by checking the local tendency to intermarriage she could lower the figures of mental deficiency, and she hoped the motor-buses would lead the people of the village to mix more with the people of the villages near. Then she's struggled always against the immorality common in a rural community; for sins of the flesh she has no tolerance or sympathy. And year by year, step by step, she's fought the devil of drunkenness. What a life, what a struggle!" He gave a little, thin laugh. "A quite indomitable woman. Yet even Miss Miall can be defeated. . . ."

As he paused I said: "I still don't see where the chimpanzees come in."

"The chimpanzees, Mr Dyke," he said, "were to be a gift to a certain nobleman, whose excellent beer we drink hereabouts, and who happens to amuse himself in his spare time with a private zoo."

"But you said she didn't like beer!"

"Ah," he said, wagging a thick finger at me, "the nobleman was to do something in return for the gift. In exchange for this valuable addition to his zoo he was to close our local pub, the Cricketers, and thus confer on this village the inestimable boon of Prohibition."

I am afraid I gaped.

The vicar smiled and said: "Precisely."

I said: "And Prohibition, as it's done in certain other places, has already brought its attendant, Crime, to East Leat." I gulped a tumblerful of water. "And you mean—you mean this is really going to happen? This brewer's going to close the pub in exchange for two chimpanzees?"

"*One*, Mr Dyke. There is only *one* chimpanzee left. I don't know if Lord Nutlin would fulfil his part of the bargain—or what Miss Miall thought was a bargain—for only one chimpanzee."

"What Miss Miall thought was a bargain?"

"I believe," he said, speaking slowly and deliberately, "there was nothing in writing. Miss Miall met Lord Nutlin some months ago and discussed the project with him. But——" He turned his big head and looked questioningly at his niece. "But it's possible, isn't it, Marion, that there may have been a slight mistake? It's possible, don't you think, that Miss Miall—dear, earnest soul that she is—may have misunderstood a beer-baron's joke?"

The girl asked harshly: "How did you find all this out?"

"But it's all quite correct, isn't it, my dear?"

"I asked, how did you find it out?"

"Well, you see," he said, "Miss Miall is the soul of fairness. As she was about to dispossess Tom Tadwell, the landlord of the Cricketers, she considered it only fair to give him warning. Further, she offered to set him up in a nice milk-bar, where he and his wife could dispense tea, coffee and milk-shakes. And poor, agitated Tom brought her letter to me. He knows very little of soft drinks and is rather distrustful of them; he has a settled prejudice that they compare unfavourably with beer. Well, I immediately took certain steps, and I was coming here this evening to discuss the matter with Miss Miall—only to find that someone else had been taking steps of a rather more drastic nature than mine. For Dr Virag's sake I am profoundly disturbed, as also for the poor animal's. But for the sake of East Leat——" He smiled round at us. "Of course," he added as an afterthought, "I do believe in temperance."

Marion Teed had got to her feet. Taking a few

steps towards the door, she turned and looked at me.

"Mr Dyke, the reason I didn't tell you all this myself was that Miss Miall had told me not to tell anyone. It wasn't that I wanted to hinder you. I want you to find out who killed the chimpanzee—in fact, I shall be very glad if you succeed in it before Miss Miall comes home. I may have been wrong in not telling you everything straight away—as I said, it was only because Miss Miall had told me to keep it entirely to myself that I didn't. I didn't know she'd told it all to Tadwell. But it's like her to think of him and the fact that he'll suffer by this change. She's always very considerate."

At that point Mrs Peach rose abruptly and went to a cupboard in the corner of the room. Marion was hesitating in the doorway; I think she wanted to add something to what she had said, something that would make us sympathetic to Rosa Miall's moral convictions instead of following the vicar's lead in irony and antagonism. But before she could speak Mrs Peach swung round.

Bright-eyed, bright-cheeked, and with her perfect features lit up by laughter, she thumped a bottle of whisky down on the table.

"Look," she cried, "look!"

Glynne jumped. His breath hissed quickly through his teeth, then he relaxed and grinned. The vicar's bloodshot eyes gleamed. Dr Virag looked puzzled. George, coming in at that moment, went to his place at the table.

"I had to," cried Mrs Peach, bubbling over, "I suddenly had to do it! I got it this evening at the local pub while you were out hunting those poor chimpanzees. I suddenly thought I couldn't be a hostess and not offer my guests something to drink. You see, I do so disagree with Aunt Rosa about all that sort of thing—and then I thought that there was a detective coming and that he'd be sure to want a lot of whisky—and then I've been living here for six months, ever since I started divorcing poor Percy, and I haven't had a single drink all that time! And also, you see——"

Glynne checked her: "Yes, Katharine, it was a very nice idea, only I hope your Aunt Rosa doesn't suddenly return." He reached for the bottle. "What about a corkscrew?"

Her face turned solemn—that is to say, it went utterly blank. Her gaze was a glassy emptiness.

"Kenneth," she said, her jaw dropping, "there isn't a corkscrew!"

"You should have thought of that," he said.

"But then it's so stupid and unnatural not to have a corkscrew in a house," she said.

"Well, what are we going to do about it?" He smiled his gentle, intimate smile into her eyes.

The vicar murmured: "So this was the mysterious parcel you were carrying when you passed me while I was resting by the roadside, Katharine?"

"Yes, I'd just been down to get it," she said. Suddenly she turned to Virag. "I don't believe I've told you yet, Dr Virag, how awful I feel about this dreadful, dreadful affair of your poor little chimpanzee. You see, I feel so specially dreadful about it because perhaps if I hadn't gone that little walk down to the village to fetch this whisky it might never have happened. I mean, the house wouldn't have been empty, and——" She gestured vaguely.

"Careful, Katharine," said Glynne with a laugh. "If you start rubbing it in too hard that you've got an alibi you'll turn into chief suspect. Now what about a corkscrew?"

In low, swift tones, looking hard at Katharine Peach, Marion Teed started speaking: "I know I'm only an employee in this house, and it isn't for me to criticise what anybody else does, even when Miss Miall's away. But there isn't really so very much difference between being paid wages for work one does and being paid an allowance for no work at all. We're both dependent on Miss Miall, Katharine. So even if I am only an employee, I'm going to say what I think." She came away from the doorway. "I think that to seize the first moment when Miss Miall's away to start doing all the things she hates, is cheap and horrid and underhand. I know how scared you'd be if she came in now and saw that bottle there. It'd make her angrier—you know it would—than anything you could do. Or almost anything. She might even be as angry as the time she gave you the sack——"

"Marion!" gasped Katharine Peach.

"Because that's what it came to, isn't it?" cried the other girl, advancing another step. She was white and rigid. "It was just giving you the sack, wasn't it? It was turning you out and stopping payment. And as she's done it once she might do it again, and if I told her——"

"Marion!" yelped the blonde woman helplessly.

"Oh, I haven't said I'm going to tell her," said Marion malevolently. "After all, there are other things I could have told her if I'd wanted to, aren't there? I never have, but I could have if I'd wanted to."

"You——!"

Mrs Peach's soft grace had gone. All tension and angles, she was bending forward over the table. Her head was poked forward, her soft lips were stretched into a tight, hard line.

Glynne broke in uncomfortably: "Marion, for God's sake——"

But Katharine Peach stopped him with a hand on his wrist. "You needn't think I'll stand it!" she cried furiously. "I've stood enough from you, you self-righteous, preaching——"

"I'll tell you what I won't stand!" Marion shouted back. "I won't stand your laughing at Miss Miall, taking advantage of her because she's away! That's one thing I'm not going to let you get away with!"

With a swift pounce she grabbed the bottle of whisky. Before anyone could stop her, she had hurled it out of the window.

Undoubtedly the vicar was the angriest.

He stared at the spot where the bottle had stood, then at the window through which it had vanished to crash with a splintering and splashing against the paved edge of one of the terraces. The yellowness of his face became suffused with purple.

"Now *that*," he shouted thickly, "is something *I*

will not stand!" He levered himself on to his feet. "That's wicked and wanton destruction—that's wicked waste. You're full of perversity, Marion. Your heart's perverse and proud. That woman you live with has dominated your will and filled you with her own pride and perversity."

Marion was holding on to a chair. Her rage, with that one violent action of flinging the bottle, had treacherously left her; its sustaining strength had gone. Weak and exhausted, she looked as if she wanted nothing but to creep from the room.

Her uncle boomed at her: "You and your Rosa Miall! Pride and perversity. . . . Impiety and puritanism. . . ." It was he who left the room. Twitching his skirts around him, and with his lips still mouthing over the words, he strode heavily away. The cold beef on his plate was unfinished. But perhaps it would have been more than he could have endured to remain so close to that shattered bottle. The spilling of God's special gift to man seemed to appear to him quite as fiendish as the spilling of Irma's life-blood had appeared to Virag.

At that point I glanced at the scientist.

His face was a mask of astonishment and disapproval. Then his lips moved slightly. No sound came from them, but only too easily I recognised the words: "I go to America and become a professor!"

* * * * *

At the time all I understood about that quarrel was that it was not about a bottle of whisky. Those two women hated each other, and the quarrel grew out of their hate. But the scene made me feel a great deal better. When suspects fall out, crimes become relatively easy to solve.

The rest of the meal would probably have been a silent one but for Katharine Peach. Sitting at one end of the oak refectory table, she talked—talked with the desperate, anxious conscientiousness of a totally unpractised person who has suddenly been moved to take seriously the responsibilities of hostess. Perhaps she thought that if only she talked continuously enough and disconnectedly enough our memories of the extraordinary scene that had taken place would become as confused as her own apparent line of thinking. Virag, to assist, suddenly gave us a dissertation on the life-history of eels. Coffee, incompetently manufactured by Mrs Peach, was served in the drawing-room.

In the light of the oil-lamps the mark on the carpet looked even larger and blacker than it had in daylight.

At a suggestion from Mrs Peach, Glynne and I rolled up the carpet and the stained underfelt and dumped them in the hall. Glynne started chatting to Marti. At once, like a cat rubbing itself against the hand that caresses it, the girl sleeked herself eagerly against his attention. She glowed with a bubbling, childish charm that had an intriguing vein of unselfconscious sensuality in it. She was warm and eager and responsive. It was rather pathetic. After a few minutes, rising, she remarked casually that she was going to take Mrs Peach's car back to the garage.

Glynne missed the suggestion. He missed it a little too obviously. Marti's mouth went sullen and her forehead creased into ugly lines. With an abrupt shrug, she walked out of the room. Feeling somewhat sorry for her, particularly when I noticed Katharine Peach's little, betraying smile, and thinking that later I might take a stroll down to the village to survey that moral battlefield, I put down my coffee-cup, three-quarters full of Mrs Peach's undrinkable coffee, and as Marti was stepping into the car I joined her.

Though I was a poor substitute for Glynne, she seemed glad of the company.

Resting a plump elbow on the steering-wheel and her rounded chin in her hand, she looked at me. " Mr Dyke, is not life a very petty and empty affair, full of people concerning themselves over sordid trifles and with nobody turning their thoughts towards the truly important, deep, beautiful things? "

" Well, that's rather what it's like sometimes," I agreed, " particularly when one's wanting something that one hasn't got. My own cures for it are drink, or some good tough stuff at the pictures, or sometimes even exercise."

" Mine's having my hair washed," she responded. But then she gave a slight shake of the head. " Only I want nothing, Mr Dyke—believe me, I want nothing."

" Well," I said, " that's fine."

" I want nothing but peace, and a few friends, and some good books, and a chance to develop my talent."

" Oh, you've got a talent? " I said. " That's nice. What is it? "

" I paint a little."

" That's very nice," I said.

" It's a great comfort, a great consolation. I really don't know where I should be without my art, Mr Dyke. Sometimes when I'm lonely, or when life seems too meaningless to me to bear thinking about at all, I think I should go mad if I hadn't an inner resource. I can always withdraw myself from the pettiness of things and concentrate on the deep and the beautiful."

I observed thoughtfully, half to myself: " I'm concentrating on something pretty deep and beautiful at the moment."

She looked at me with surprising sharpness. " *I* don't think Mrs Peach is at all deep, I think she's quite stupid, and, as a matter of fact, I don't think she's really beautiful. I think she's too pale and thin."

I laughed, and Marti, frowning, studied me searchingly.

" Mr Dyke, you are a very intelligent man—are you really going to stay here wasting your time about this silly little problem? "

" Don't you want me to, Marti? "

" It is of absolutely no concern to me."

" Well," I said, " I'm glad to hear it, because I'd far sooner a nice girl like you wasn't concerned in it."

" But are you really going to——? "

" I'm afraid so."

She gave her head a regretful shake. Still eyeing

me, she settled back in her seat. "I'm so sorry—so very sorry to see you waste your gifts on this silly little problem."

"Why d'you call it a silly little problem, Marti? I think it's rather a nice one."

"But I feel so certain you've great gifts, Mr Dyke. . . . Haven't there been any real murders recently, any real, human murders on which you could show how really remarkable your abilities are?"

"Probably lots," I answered, "but the police seem to be getting along all right without me."

"It's a pity," she said, "it's a great pity."

She leant her head against the back of her seat. She stared up at the sky. She did it at first with a calculated soulfulness that was meant to show me how she could withdraw herself from human stupidity and smallness to contemplation of the night's dark, star-filled depth. But after a moment that expression faded, leaving simple moodiness on her young, rather bitter face.

I said: "What about taking the car down to the garage?"

She took no notice.

I said: "Well, Marti, may I ask you a question?"

"What is it?" she asked with a sigh.

"That scene that happened at supper, that quarrel —have there been others like it since you've been here?"

She took her time to answer the simple question. Turning her head as it rested against the back of the seat, she looked into my face again and I noticed that her teeth were clamped over her lower lip and that there were small, deep lines between her brows.

Suddenly she jerked herself upright and nodded at me emphatically.

"Yes," she said, "yes, there have been quarrels—many of them."

"Between Mrs Peach and Miss Teed?"

"Oh, and Father Teed too—oh, between everyone, only not Dr Glynne. Dr Glynne's nature is above such petty quarrelling. Didn't you see how deeply upset and embarrassed he was by that horrid scene?"

"Yes," I said, "yes—I saw it."

"But indeed, there've been many scenes like it, exactly like it," she said with animation. "In the morning, in the afternoon, in the evening—they happen at any time, in any place. It's *most* unpleasant. Suddenly to have all one's thoughts disarranged by those two women screaming at one another, and to have that happen again and again—you've no idea how distressing it is, how—well, how ashamed for them it makes one feel, and also how worn out. I'm so very sensitive, you see; it makes me suffer dreadfully. They're altogether shameless and ill-bred, Mr Dyke, both of them. However much I hated another person, I should never have the rudeness to make such scenes in front of my visitors—and all day too, every day. You ask me, have there been such scenes before? . . . Oh, Mr Dyke, if I were to tell you all I've heard——"

"If you were to tell me the truth, Marti, I'd like it even better."

"The truth? This is the truth, Mr Dyke! But believe me," she went on earnestly, "only a little of it. Why, I've only just begun to tell you——"

"You've only just begun to tell me a little of the gorgeous fiction your mind's busy on at the moment, making it bigger and brighter every instant. My dear girl," I said, "it's part of my job to smell a lie."

"If you think I am lying you have a very bad sense of smell, Mr Dyke!"

"Listen," I said, "the first thing to learn if you're out to take people in is not to overdo things. Caution and under-statement are the basis of effective lying—of *tête-à-tête* lying, that's to say. Naturally from public platforms it's another matter."

"But I never tell lies, never! I'm a completely sincere person, I hate and abominate all kinds of deception, I regard——"

"I know, you regard truth and sincerity as sacred things, and you're careful to keep at a respectful distance from them. Very well, it's quite all right, if you enjoy it. But I've no use for a lie at the moment, I want to know the truth."

"The truth—I've told you nothing but the truth!" She was beating her clenched fists against one another, and working herself up; I recognised the symptoms. "Oh, if there's a thing I hate, it's a person who's mean and small and distrustful, a person who never believes what they cannot understand, a person who——"

"For heaven's sake. . . . Listen, I can understand

everything you've told me. It's simple a, b, c. Only it isn't true."

" It is all true ! "

" Suppose we get on to the garage."

" It is true ! "

After that there were several minutes of hysterical protestations and denunciations. I was at a disadvantage because earlier that evening I had been mistaken in my disbelief. All the same, I knew she was lying to me. I was not certain to what extent she was lying; it might be true that she had seen the hate between the two women flare up more than once; even of that, however, I was doubtful. That she had not witnessed what she said she had I was sure. After some argument I managed to silence her into sulks, and at last, with a face of stubborn anger, she drove the car down to the garage.

As I got out of the car to open the garage doors she spoke again: " What I cannot understand is, *why* you should think I'm lying, Mr Dyke." Her tone had become elaborately reasonable.

" Can't you, Marti ? "

" No, indeed I can't. I've never been anything but sincere and open with you, yet you distrusted me from the first minute you saw me. I know you did—I can always tell when a person distrusts me."

" Does it happen so often ? "

" Please . . . I don't want to quarrel with you, I want to be quite fair-minded. If I could comprehend your distrust of me perhaps I shouldn't feel so hurt by it."

"I'm sorry you feel hurt by it. You shouldn't, you know; it isn't a serious matter."

"But it is—to me it is very serious. I can't bear being distrusted."

"Well, the cure's quite easy. But I don't think your lies are so awfully serious. I think they're just a habit, something you do without thinking about it. Probably you feel people won't pay you enough attention if you stick to the not-very-interesting truth. I think you've got it into your head that you're a rather neglected person—that your father, for instance, neglects you for the sake of his chimpanzees, and for all I know, you may be perfectly right about that, but the fact is——"

"Oh, I think you're a horrible man!" she burst out. "You're horrible and vicious! I think I've never in my whole life disliked anyone as much as I do you. It's unforgivable, the way you act towards me. I shall tell my father about it. If I were not so well-bred and controlled I should slap your face. In fact, I think perhaps it would be a good thing to do anyhow. In fact, I think perhaps I shall!"

"Go ahead," I said.

"Oh, you're horrible and detestable! As if I should! But you misunderstand me on purpose, and then you say I'm lying to you. You'll say it's a lie, I suppose, because I said I should slap your face and didn't, when in fact I should never dream of any action so undignified. I dislike all forms of violence. I don't suppose a person like you can understand that; your life is made up of blood and horrors, you expect everyone you meet to have a knife up his sleeve. But I believe that people should be kind and liberal to one another, and that trust, unquestioning trust, is the only basis of friendship." She had jabbered at me until she thought I was off my guard; she chose that moment to lash at me, open-handed, across the face.

When she had done it she glared at me with big, rather frightened eyes. Then she went pallidly subdued. She climbed out of the car.

"You can put the car away yourself," she muttered. "I can't be bothered with it."

"All right," I said.

She took a few steps along the road. I had the garage doors open; as I got into the car again she stood still and looked back at me.

"Well," she said defiantly, "why didn't you do anything about it?"

"About what?"

"About my slapping you."

"I dislike all forms of violence."

She turned and walked off towards the house. I drove the car forward into the garage.

It was as I was closing and locking the doors of the garage that I heard a chuckle nearby and saw the tip of a cigarette glowing in the darkness.

"Well, now you're getting acquainted with the kid. Good company, isn't she?" said Ingham.

He was standing in the doorway of the building that housed Leofric; he had one shoulder propped against the doorframe and his hands in his pockets. As I went towards him I could see the grin on his face.

He went on: "You know, she did that to me once, and for more or less the same reason. I'd been telling her in some detail why I found it difficult to believe that her old man was in the habit of shutting her up and feeding her on bread and water whenever he was annoyed with her, and then I went into some more details about why it gave her so much satisfaction to pretend that he did. She waited till she got her chance, then she walloped me across the face, the same way she did you. Only I acted with less restraint than you did; I turned her the other way up and gave it her a lot better than she'd given it."

"Then she must have been pretty disappointed in me."

"Mind you, it isn't her fault; she's never had much of a chance," said Ingham. "The old man hasn't the faintest notion of what's going on in that kid."

"Any more excitements down here tonight?" I inquired.

"All quiet so far," he replied.

"I've been giving some thought to the lay-out around here," I said. "You can see these buildings from the house. It's struck me that when you went off to fetch your cigarettes this evening, someone from the house must have seen you go."

"I guess they must've. I wasn't gone long," he answered.

"And you've no idea who it might have been?"

"I don't have to share my ideas with anyone."

"I'm not forgetting," I said, "that the first time Irma and Leofric were let out of their cages was in London, when, so far as we know, only you and Dr Virag and Miss Virag were present."

"Weren't you with Dr Virag and the girl yourself when Irma was killed?" Ingham asked quietly.

"I was," I replied.

He sucked in some smoke. I saw him pout his lips and expel the smoke again in short puffs that hung above him in the motionless air.

"Listen," he said after a moment, speaking without excitement or rancour, "I know I'm the one it looks to you must've done it. I'm not protesting; I know that's the way the facts make it look."

"If I knew just what you'd gain by it," I said, "I'd certainly agree with you."

"Well, I'm not going to start telling you that the boss is someone to whom I owe a great deal and for whom I'd go a long way out of my way if it'd please him any. That's just the kind of thing I'd be bound to say if I was the one who'd done it. All I'm going to say is, can you point to any conceivable way that I'd benefit by doing a crazed thing like killing Irma? If Virag goes to the States, as he'll have to if he doesn't get the money, I'm likely to be out of a job, that's all."

"Wouldn't he take you with him?"

"He might—but I mightn't go."

"America not being necessarily the healthiest spot for such a phoney American?"

He turned his head and looked at me. In the

same quiet tone he asked: "Is it anything to you where I happen to come from?"

"Not that I know of," I said.

"Then suppose you keep off the subject."

"Can you give me something more interesting to think about?"

"I certainly can!"

The swiftness, the emphasis of the reply startled me. I had expected my question to be turned aside again with a retort that it wasn't a part of his job to occupy my mind. But for once he seemed to have something that he was eager to say.

With his head sunk between his broad shoulders and his cigarette dangling from his lips, he said: "I've just been putting this problem to that friend of yours who brought me my meal. You see, there's something that's been puzzling me ever since I found Leofric over there in the wood. When it turned out Irma was in the house I was still more puzzled. It's something that wouldn't strike any of the others, perhaps not even Virag, because even Virag doesn't know these chimps the way I do. I know them as you know people. I know their characters, their little kinks, the things they're afraid of, the things that make them savage, the things that'll calm them down. I shouldn't be surprised if I'm a lot more intimate with them than I've ever been with a human being. And so when they go and act against their characters it surprises me just as much as it would you if one of your friends suddenly returned a book he'd borrowed, or if your bank-manager sent you an invitation to overdraw. You see, it ought to have been Irma who was in the wood and Leofric who was in the house."

I said: "I don't follow."

Quickly, seriously, and without troubling to put the accent into his voice, he went on: "I told you earlier that it was always Irma who went off and disappeared, while Leofric was always found close to the cages. Irma was always the skittish one; she was much the friendlier, much the more active. Leofric's the more intelligent; he always got the better results in Virag's experiments, also he isn't as easily frightened by strange things. When we once put a toy dog in the cage Irma nearly had a nervous breakdown, but Leofric got acquainted with it and even learnt how to make it squeak. He's always interested too if you take him for a ride in a car, whereas Irma's scared out of her wits. But Leofric's too lazy or too meditative or something to try to get around himself. And so it's all wrong that he should have been in the wood—because that wood'd be a good distance off even for Irma—while Irma should only have trotted up to the house and got herself stabbed there. It's all wrong, I tell you. I know you can't check what I'm saying, because you don't know the chimps, and so I might be making the whole thing up to confuse you. But it's all wrong—it's really all wrong. So if you're puzzling about me and Virag and Marti, and all the other people up at the house, you should do some puzzling about Irma and Leofric too. And then come and tell me, when you've worked it out, why those two chimps have acted right out of character."

*   *   *   *   *

Presently I strolled down into the village.

A dark triangle of grass for a village green, one or two narrow streets of old houses, dimly lit by a few lamps, a squat church and silence, that was all there was to it at that hour of the evening. No one came or went. East Leat in the starlight was an eerie place.

I can give no reasons for that impression of eeriness. Perhaps it was not East Leat that was eerie, but simply the thoughts that rushed into my mind as soon as I was alone.

For it was as I was walking across the deserted green, with a skyline of old roofs and yew trees ahead of me, and with the faint yowling of a cat in the darkness the only sound I could hear, that the peculiar unpleasantness of the crime I was there to investigate, the twisted fury of that stabbing and all that it told of vicious distortion in some human brain, really became clear to me. I wondered, was there somebody mad up at that house on the hill—or merely coldly, selfishly ruthless? Or was it something else, something even uglier, more sinister? . . .

As a cat brushed past my ankles and its dark shape leapt up on to a wall, doubt and disgust and a queer uneasiness jostled against my more rational thoughts. I saw again that long, red tongue of blood across the carpet, and the crumpled, hairy body. . . .

I felt more unsure of myself than usual. I had

never before had to solve a problem of crime where the solution might rest on understanding correctly the characters of two chimpanzees. I wanted to laugh at it—and instead found I was suffering from the horrors.

Looking back, it seems natural to wonder if I was having an attack of intuition.

Suddenly a man blundered past me in the darkness. In a thick, throaty voice, beerily benign, he greeted me: " There's nothin' like Nutlin's! "

Startled but, for the moment, reassured, I turned back towards 2 Titmore Lane.

I realised I had just encountered a man who had established, to his own satisfaction, one of the eternal verities.

—— IV ——

GEORGE AND I were in our bedroom. George was already in bed. I was sitting near the open french window, looking out into the garden. The room was lit only by the one candle we had been given, too faint for even a small arc of light to fall on the grass outside. I had just been telling George what I had learnt of Rosa Miall's reason for wanting the chimpanzees, and George had given it as his opinion that the old lady was crackers. I agreed with him and I had no desire to bring Prohibition to East Leat. But I did want to help Dr Virag.

" I've got an idea, the dim beginning of a theory," I said, " but the trouble is, there's too much missing still."

" That's right," said George, " the old lady's missin'."

" And the bloodstains," I said. " There must have been bloodstains on somebody's hands or clothing. Yet they're missing."

" Gettin' quite interested in the case, ain't you, Tobe? " said George. " Almost as if it really was murder."

" I like Virag. I want him to get his money," I said.

" I reckon you've forgotten already how much you didn't like his letter."

"Shut up. I like him, I tell you. I want him to get that money. But there's someone who wants to make it damned difficult for him to get it."

"Then you and me are goin' to stay and make it damned difficult for that person to make it damned difficult?"

"That's it," I said.

George closed his eyes. He asked drowsily: "Anyone special you're fancyin' at the moment?"

I did not answer. "The trouble is," I said, "that we know that whoever did the killing must have got blood on to himself. The fact's certain. But no one we've seen had any blood on hands or clothing. Incidentally, the only people who haven't got alibis now are Ingham and Marion Teed. But those are just the two for whom I can't find any reasonable motive."

"Suppose Ingham was bribed," said George, "then he wouldn't need any motive—any motive of his own like."

"I've been doing a good deal of thinking about Ingham," I said, "but he wasn't bribed—he's too fond of the animals."

"Then what about Miss Teed?"

"I'd have liked to get a talk with her tonight," I said, "but she was too wrought up; it wouldn't have done any good. Yet it's clear she's the only person here who really likes Miss Miall and approves of her schemes. So why should she want to smash up the schemes by stabbing one of the chimpanzees?"

"Maybe she's goin' to inherit some of Miss Miall's money," said George. "Or maybe she's been embezzlin' some of it already and don't want the sort of account-takin' there'd be if a big lump of it went to Virag. Or maybe her mind's warped and she just likes killin' things. Or maybe she's fallen in love with Virag and killed his chimp because he spurned her. Or——"

" Shut up."

" I'm just tryin' to help, Tobe. I reckon I can find you plenty more motives if you want 'em—I kind of got the knack of it."

" Shut up, I'm trying to think," I said.

George stayed silent. I got up and began to undress. The whole house was quiet and the night outside had a hot, tired stillness. I was too tired myself to think properly. When I tried to push my mind at the problem Ingham had put to me of why the two chimpanzees had acted out of character, I could not get my teeth into it. The headache which the journey to Bule had given me had come back, and I had no aspirins.

It was when I had been in bed about five minutes that a sound, which drowsiness at first made me confuse with my own thoughts, came softly to my hearing.

The sound came from the open window.

For a moment, sleepily, I tried to dismiss it, then I sat up, listened carefully, and as I realised that it was the sound of lowered voices, I got up and crossed the room. By standing at one side of the window where the blue curtain hung I could, without risk of being seen, look out into the garden through a chink between the curtain and the window-frame. I saw the dark curve of the hilltop against the starry sky. I saw the deep, shadowed hollow of the garden with its ghostly walls of chalk. I saw that there were two people on the bench in the little garden. They were sitting close together and I could see the profile of the one who was nearer to me. It was Kenneth Glynne.

It was Glynne who was speaking. His voice was lowered, but the words were clearly spoken.

"But, why, why? Why shouldn't people know? Why shouldn't everyone know? What is there to hide?"

I did not catch the answer. It was a woman's voice, but the words came too whisperingly for me to be able to recognise to whom the voice belonged. I could not see whom it was either; she had a dark scarf over her hair and was wearing a coat of some dark material; I could see a knee, the tip of a shoe, a shoulder.

"Why?" Glynne repeated. There was a brusque note of irritation in his voice. "I can't understand it. I'd like everyone to know about it. I'm—I'm proud about it, and I want everyone to see that I am."

Again the woman murmured. Glynne stirred restlessly and I saw that nervous gesture of his as he thrust a hand through his hair. "I'm damned if I understand—I'm damned if I even want to understand. Secrecy's hell; it takes the edge off everything."

The woman sighed, saying nothing.

"The only possible reason for it," he went on

fiercely, "is that you don't feel certain of your feeling for me, that you know you don't really love me. Well, why not say so? You've said bad things to me before now; you've tackled every damned fault in my character. Why not go on and tell me that the real trouble is you don't love me? You don't have to go on with it if you don't want to. You can break it off and—after all, that was the point of the secrecy, wasn't it?—you can break it off and no one can spread misleading stories that it's you who've been let down, you who've been made a fool of."

The woman whispered a few words.

Glynne exclaimed furiously: "What a fool you are! Why can't I make you understand—why don't you believe me? *I* not love *you*! My God, if only you'd——"

She interrupted with an ironic laugh.

Glynne caught hold of her by the shoulders and swung her round to face him. As he held her like that, away from him at first, then jerking her forward and pressing his mouth down on hers, I saw her face. It looked very white; the eyes in the darkness were only hollows of expressionless shadow, but the mouth had a tight, hurt look. It was a shock to me to realise who it was, because I had been taking for granted as I listened that it was somebody different.

It was Marion Teed.

After a moment the girl said: "It's all a lot of fuss about nothing, anyhow, because everyone knows. I haven't told a single person we're going to be married, yet—everyone knows."

"*I* haven't told anyone," said Glynne quickly.

" Except Katharine," said Marion.

" We agreed about that, didn't we? We agreed she'd have to be told."

" Yes—and now everyone knows."

" Well, why the hell shouldn't they? "

" You see, Kenneth," she said slowly, hesitating between the words as if she were choosing each one deliberately, " I've had a—a certain idea about you for some time. I'm not sure even now that—that I'm wrong. It's the sort of idea that—poisons one's mind. So let's just wait a little longer and see. . . ."

Glynne laughed. Pushing his fingers through his hair again, he sat staring up at the line between hill-top and sky.

" You know, Marion," he said, " if you do make up your mind that you're fed up with me, or that you never really wanted me at all—put it just how you like—then I shan't have to worry any longer, shall I, about your prohibition on Dr Virag and his chimpanzees? I can return to the subject of the nice, long, interesting talk I had with him the other evening—I mean when I was telling him about the work I did on chimpanzees at Oxford. Of course, I've been wanting to; it was only because of what you said to me afterwards that I let it drop—that I even damped it down when Virag showed signs of getting back to it yesterday evening. You see, I know I made a good impression on him, and that he was more than half serious when he said that I ought to be doing his sort of work. I'm pretty sure that with a little encouragement I could get him to ask me to go to Tobago. He told me one of his assistants is leaving soon, so there'd be a vacancy. And if you don't want me——"

"Not want you!" she said in a thin, shaking voice. "Why d'you have to keep twisting it like that when you know that I—when you know that the trouble is . . . ? Oh, if you don't want to understand. . . . Of course, you can do just what you like about Dr Virag. I wasn't putting a pro-hibition on anything. I was only saying that I think your own work is the finest sort of work there is, but that's only my opinion and of course you're free to do anything you like. If you really want to go to Tobago, and if—if we ever really get married, then of course I should be ready to go with you, only——"

"Only you don't intend me to go, do you?" said Glynne quietly.

She stared at him, and Glynne, looking into her face, laughed again.

"All right, Marion," he said, "I won't go."

She looked away from him and said in a dreary tone: "I'm very tired; perhaps I'm being rather stupid about everything."

"You are, rather," he said.

"You oughtn't to have stayed and made me talk. I've made a bad enough fool of myself already this evening."

Glynne hesitated, then he got to his feet.

"All right. Good night, Marion. Don't worry, I don't really mean that about going to Tobago."

"It's not about that I'm worrying," she said.

" I expect I'll look in some time in the morning," he went on.

" Of course—to look at Katharine's hand."

" You're an awful fool, Marion."

" Perhaps."

He stooped and kissed her once more, then walked off rapidly. He did not go round the house, but up the side of the chalk cutting and then away over the edge of the hill. Marion Teed sat where she was for a moment, then she began quietly to cry. She was crying as she disappeared into the house through another of its french windows.

As I felt my way back to bed I was cursing; I don't enjoy listening to scenes like that. But also I was reflecting on the fact that Marion Teed appeared to have a reason for wishing that Dr Virag's experimental station should have to close down.

Out of the darkness a moment later George spoke through a yawn: " Rum thing, Tobe—when I realised it was the doctor out there and that he was talkin' love to some woman or other, I kind of leapt to the conclusion it was Mrs Peach."

" Oh? " I said. " So did I."

" Rum," George repeated. " I suppose it was just that it never struck me a bloke like him, that's probably got plenty of opportunities, could fall for that chip off the good old ice-block. Of course, she's got more brains than Mrs Peach, but Mrs Peach has got a lot more of a lot of the other things."

" It's Mrs Peach he's in love with, and that girl knows it." I lay scowling at the ceiling. " Has it struck you that in this house there are three women in love with the same man?"

"And yet it's a chimpanzee that goes and gets murdered!"

"But why the hell do they have to come and make a scene like that right outside my bedroom window?" I asked angrily. "I've got to listen. I'm paid to listen and to look and to find out all I can. But when it means listening in to that sort of thing I don't like it. So why the hell do they have to go and do it where I damn well can't help overhearing the whole of it?"

I heard George roll over in bed.

"Myself," he said, "I'd never dream of talkin' to my girl with a snoop like you anywhere in the neighbourhood, unless of course——"

"Unless what?"

"Unless," said George through another yawn, "I'd some reason for wanting you to overhear it all, Tobe. . . ."

*　　*　　*　　*　　*

I had told George I was developing a theory, but it was not until next morning that I began to realise how much I liked my theory.

Lighting myself a cigarette—for the austere shadow of Rosa Miall could not prevent my smoking in bed—I propped my head up to help clear the drowsiness out of it, and prepared to do some hard thinking. George had got up and gone out without waking me; he had even made his bed.

The question was, where had the gloves and the apron or other covering that Irma's killer must have worn been hidden?

Unfortunately they had probably been destroyed during the night, so the fact that I felt pretty certain where they must have been hidden before their destruction was not very helpful. Yet it was possible that the killer had been careless. It was not, after all, a human being he had stabbed, and if the crime was discovered he would not be hanged by the neck until he was dead. So perhaps he had not troubled to do more than bundle the bloodstained objects out of sight, in which case it would be worth while searching for them. Certainly, if I could find them, particularly if I found them in the place where I believed them to be, it would simplify the matter of proof.

I smoked another two cigarettes. When I came downstairs to a late breakfast there was no one but Katharine Peach in the dining-room.

She was sitting with both elbows on the table, sipping abstractedly at a cup of black coffee. In a white, sleeveless dress she looked more ethereal than ever. Telling me in her soft, blurry voice to help myself, she returned to her unfocused contemplation of a spot on the bare wall opposite. The morning was fresh and clear, with sunshine pouring in at the open window, though puddles on the terraces showed that it had rained fairly heavily some time during the night.

Whenever I looked at Katharine Peach it was the bandage on her hand that caught my eye. She was holding her cup in both hands, cradling it between the palms. The bandage on her hand left only the tips of the fingers showing.

After a little I inquired: " How did you hurt your hand, Mrs Peach? "

She came out of her thoughts with a start. She smiled at me. "Oh, I just cut it a little a few days ago."

" And it festered? "

" If ever I cut myself it always festers."

" That's nasty," I said.

" Oh, it is," she said, " it really is. Kenneth says my constitution's simply rotten. In fact "—she widened her blue eyes at me like a child—" in fact, he says I'm rotten right through. Me, he means, you know—me myself."

" That's nasty too," I said.

Crossing to the sideboard, she poured out another cup of coffee.

" That friend of yours is so obliging," she said. " He's taken the carpet to the cleaner's for us. Have you had any good ideas about the whole thing, Mr Dyke? It's such an extraordinary thing to happen, isn't it? Of course, you know, Kenneth's quite right —I mean about me. But then he's so terribly perspicacious, I always think. Don't you think he's awfully intelligent? Dr Virag does."

I sipped some of my own coffee. It was so good this morning that I knew George had helped with the making of it.

" Why does Glynne think you're rotten right through? " I asked. But it was the carpet I was thinking about. I was wondering what George had actually done with the thing. " I don't see at the moment why that should recommend anyone's intelligence."

" But then you don't know me as well as Kenneth does, do you? "

" Total rottenness, all the same, is a rather sweeping assertion."

" You're just trying to be nice to me," she said, with a sudden, wonderful smile that would have cleft me right through if it had happened, say, after lunch; luckily, at breakfast I am receptive to nothing but food.

She went on gravely : "You know, whenever I start thinking about myself seriously—but you don't want me to talk about myself, do you, Mr Dyke? You'd far sooner talk about the chimpanzees."

" I've an idea that the affair of the chimpanzees is going to need only a very little more of my attention," I said, " so please go on."

" Really? " she asked eagerly. " Oh, how marvellous. It's such a horrid cloud hanging over us. . . . Well, you see, whenever I start thinking about myself seriously, I always come to the conclusion that Kenneth's perfectly right. There's my stupidity to begin with. People oughtn't to be stupid, ought they? I think it's just as bad as—well, all the other things I am. Ungrateful, for instance. Aunt Rosa's always saying I'm ungrateful. You know Aunt Rosa adopted me, don't you? That's something I ought to be very, very grateful about, isn't it? "

I reached for some toast. " I should say that depends."

" Well "—and her tone went suddenly sombre— " I *am* grateful." Abstracted melancholy settled on her face. Taking a sip of her black coffee, she added softly : " I am really *very* grateful."

133

I put butter and marmalade on the toast and went on with my breakfast.

Katharine Peach let her bandaged hand drop on to her lap.

She murmured sadly: "Then look at the sort of person I fall in love with. I mean to say, look at poor Percy. I really and truly did fall most terribly in love with poor Percy. Aunt Rosa says it means I'm depraved. D'you think it does?"

"Possibly—only I've never met poor Percy."

She widened her eyes at me again. "Of course you haven't! How silly of me. Well, Percy's a bad, immoral man whom I've got to divorce, and he drinks and he's dishonest, and he isn't even handsome any more—he's got fat, you know, and his skin's getting that sort of spongy look."

"Poor, poor Percy."

"Yes, *I* think he's so much to be pitied," she said, sighing, "but Aunt Rosa can't see it. He used to be so terribly handsome, you see—though, as a matter of fact, Aunt Rosa couldn't see that either. If you talk to her about a man being handsome, she always says she thinks Mr Gladstone had a very striking face. Well, Percy was never at all like Mr Gladstone, he was altogether too sort of South American looking, and of course that appealed to me terribly; you know what I mean, sleek black hair and olive skin and a sort of slithery way of walking as if he did it by flapping fins instead of feet. Whenever I watched him walking it used to turn me completely into a jelly. I suppose that's what Aunt Rosa thought so depraved. . . . But I always talk too much about myself, don't I? And I know that in spite of what you say, you'd sooner be talking about the chimpanzees." She sighed. " Poor Percy, I sometimes think I love him still, only Aunt Rosa's so awfully right about its being impossible for me to go on living with him. Dear Aunt Rosa. Percy simply hates her, of course. He was simply furious when she refused to let me have an allowance after I married him."

It was at that point in the conversation that I suddenly began to wonder whether Katharine Peach was carefully directing her flow of babble so as to put me in possession of certain facts. But her small face was as vague and innocent as usual.

" Now do ask me something about the chimpanzees, Mr Dyke," she said. " I'm sure you'd be asking me all sorts of questions if I were giving you a chance, but I do all the talking myself. Not that I can tell you anything; if I were a sensible person like Marion or Kenneth I'd be able to tell you lots, I expect, but I never seem to know anything about anything. Of course, you know Marion and Kenneth are engaged to be married? "

" Indeed? " I said.

" Yes, they've been engaged for a whole week— only I mustn't talk about it, it's a secret. Now can't you ask me something about the chimpanzees so that I can feel I'm being useful? "

She waited a moment while I went on eating; then, with a slightly disappointed air, she got started again on her own.

" Perhaps there's something I ought to tell you, Mr Dyke. You know when you were asking us at dinner last night if any of us knew why Aunt Rosa wanted the chimpanzees and I said I didn't know? Well, that wasn't absolutely, strictly true. I did know. But people don't expect me to know things, so it was quite easy for me to say that I didn't, and, you see, I had two perfectly good reasons for saying that I didn't. First, you see, I'm afraid of Marion. You saw what sort of a temper she's got, and she's always trying to make difficulties for me with Aunt Rosa. Well, I knew that if I said anything about it she'd be simply furious with me. And the second reason was that... Well, it's difficult to explain, but I'm very fond of Aunt Rosa really, and yet I can't help feeling that her whole scheme's so very, very absurd, and I just didn't want to say anything that'd make her sound stupid in front of strangers. D'you understand? "

" I suppose so," I said. " But your discretion might have been rather hard on Dr Virag, mightn't it? "

" How? " She looked puzzled.

" Suppose no one had given me the information."

" Yes? "

" Suppose that had prevented my finding out who stabbed Irma."

" Oh, but it couldn't make any difference to Dr Virag—I mean about his getting the money for his experimental place. He's delivered the chimpanzees and so he'll get his money. Aunt Rosa said so herself. And it's only right that he should—unless he'd something to do with killing Irma himself, and I can't believe that, because if he had had he wouldn't have a detective here now trying to find out who'd done it, would he? He'd be only too glad to leave it all to Sawbry. Oh no, it won't make any difference to Dr Virag."

Suddenly I was interested in her conversation. " And how many people know that, Mrs Peach— that it won't make any difference to Dr Virag? "

" Everyone, I should think. I mean, everyone knows that Aunt Rosa's the soul of fairness, so that——"

" But how many people *know*? "

" Well, I know—and Aunt Rosa—and Marion."

" Does Dr Virag himself know? "

" Well, I heard Aunt Rosa telling him he should have the money."

" Thank you, Mrs Peach," I said. " Thank you very much indeed."

" Oh, have I managed to tell you something you wanted to know? "

" You certainly have."

She beamed at me.

I got up in a hurry and went looking for George. I wanted to tell him all about my theory.

*   *   *   *   *

George was not in the kitchen where I had expected to find him. Only Marion Teed was there, shelling peas. She told me that George had taken the carpet to the cleaner's. It appeared he had also helped her with cooking the breakfast and with peeling the potatoes for lunch. There was a slight warming of the cold voice when the girl spoke of George But when I, thinking it might be a good idea to imitate his technique and get a little of her confidence, started shelling peas, she immediately thanked me briskly and, snatching a mop and duster out of the cupboard, went flying off upstairs.

I was near the end of the peas when George strolled into the kitchen.

"Hullo—up already?" he said sarcastically.

Reaching over my shoulder he picked a pea out of the basin and ate it.

"Don't do that, they aren't yours," I said. "Now what's all this about a carpet?"

"I just taken it down to the cleaner's," he said.

"I know you've just taken it down to the cleaner's. Everyone's been telling me so. But why? That carpet may be an important piece of evidence."

"Sure, Tobe. But if I hadn't taken it somebody else would've."

"What d'you mean?"

"Just what I'm sayin'. The police hadn't told them they wasn't to have the carpet cleaned, so what good was it tryin' to stop them? And they was all mighty set on havin' it cleaned, so I just said I'd take it along for them."

"Oh, you just said you'd take it along for them. George, what have you done with that carpet?"

"Taken it to the cleaner's, Tobe."

"Listen, George," I said, knocking his hand out of the way as he reached for another pea, "have you taken into consideration the kind of woman Rosa Miall appears to be? I don't see her as one of those gentle, understanding, forgiving women. If anything happens to that carpet——"

"But all I done is take it to the cleaner's, Tobe! Look!" He thrust a slip of paper down on the table before me. It was a cleaner's receipt for one carpet.

I groaned. "Why the devil didn't you hide the thing or something? Sending off evidence to the cleaner's! You don't usually do damn fool things like that."

I was so annoyed, I almost made up my mind not to discuss my theory with him.

But I wanted to hear how good it sounded.

First I explained why I no longer placed Mrs Peach at the head of the list of suspects and so had lost interest in her. Mrs Peach had an alibi, and the motive which had drawn my attention to her apparently did not exist. I gave George as lucid an account as I could of her conversation, and pointed out that if Miss Miall had promised Dr Virag his money on delivery of the animals, there could be no advantage, from Mrs Peach's point of view, in killing one of the apes, since the money was lost to her anyhow.

Then I went on to Teed. The vicar was the person who had shown the most violent feelings about the chimpanzees. He had shaken his fist at the empty cages; he detested the purpose which the animals were to serve. Also his feelings of friendliness towards Miss Miall were, to put it mildly, very superficial.

However, I did not believe that the vicar had stabbed Irma. He was a fleshy, flabby man and he was ill; he was ill enough to need a rest by the roadside every time he came up the hill to see Miss Miall. But if he had stabbed Irma and then, interrupted in moving her by our arrival, had had to get away in a hurry, he would have had to jump out of the window and run down the hillside at great speed. I did not believe he was capable of it.

"Besides," I said, "the first attempt at theft happened in London. That points clearly at Virag himself, or Marti, or Ingham. But Virag and Marti were in the car with us when Irma was killed."

George said with a frown: "I said to you last night, maybe Ingham was bribed to do it."

"Not bribed," I said. "His respect for Virag is real; I don't believe he'd go back on him for money. But Ingham's a man with a secret—and Teed knows that secret. Ingham's got something he's trying to hide under a false accent, a false nationality, and probably a false name. Teed knows his real name, and where he comes from, and what he's done. And somehow, I believe, Teed must have got to know that this man over whom he has power was working for Virag. Teed threatened—Ingham gave in. I'm pretty sure the act itself is Ingham's, but the man behind it is the worthy vicar of East Leat."

Irritatingly, George went back to the first few remarks I had made. "You don't have to pay too much attention to that alibi of Mrs Peach's, Tobe."

"Why not?"

"I've discovered there's two ways down to the village. D'you remember the way the doctor went home last night, up over the top of the hill? There's a path goes down there and it's quicker than by the road. So if she'd bolted down that way——"

"Don't be a fool. She couldn't have heard us arriving, dropped Irma, jumped out of the window, raced down to the village getting rid of the blood-stains on the way, bought the whisky at the pub, walked up the hill past the vicar and got back to the house at the time that she did."

"That's true, Tobe. But suppose it was somethin' else that interrupted her. Suppose Irma'd been shifted ten minutes or more before we arrived. Or suppose she wasn't shifted. Suppose we haven't hit on the right reason for the stain of blood bein' the shape it was."

"Well, what other reason can you think of?"

He scratched his head. "I got some ideas floatin' around, but they ain't definite. . . . Still, suppose we haven't got the right reason."

"The only supposing I'm doing at the minute is that Teed forced Ingham to kill that chimpanzee, that when Ingham heard us arriving he jumped out of the window and raced down the hill, that he gave Teed, who was waiting by the road, the bloodstained gloves and apron, that Teed hid them under his skirts and took them back to the vicarage with him last night—and that that's where we may be able to find them, or at least the charred remnants of them. And you and I are now going looking for them."

"No, Tobe," said George, crunching another raw pea, "I'm afraid——"

I cut him short. "Look here, I've just been telling you, Virag knows that he's going to get his money. Well, think how Virag's attitude to this crime backs up my theory. He can't make up his mind whether he wants you and me to stay and find out what really happened, or whether he wants to pack up and go straight off to America. Virag's not a fool. He knows that the first attack on the chimps having happened in London points to one of his own party being guilty. Well, he's a scrupulous person, and if it turns out that it's one of his own party that's guilty he won't take the money. But he's human also, and so at one moment he thinks it'd be best to go away quick before anything's been proved, then the next moment he thinks no, it's his duty to stay and help arrive at the truth."

" Yes, yes, but all I was goin' to say was, about the gloves and apron——"

" Well? "

" Well, there weren't any gloves and apron, Tobe."

" There must have been. And you're coming along to the vicarage now to see if you can find an opportunity, while I'm talking to Teed, of getting in and having a good search for them."

" I'll go anywhere you like and look for anything you like," said George, " only not for something that can't be there. And so instead of goin' to the vicarage I reckon you better come along with me and have a chat with a new pal of mine who's got something pretty surprisin' to tell you."

" What new pal? "

George picked up a milk-bottle and put it down on the corner of the receipt for the carpet to prevent the slip of paper being blown off the table while we were gone.

He answered: " He's a mighty important bloke, I reckon. It's Leofric."

*   *   *   *   *

Leofric was not in his cage but having a game with Ingham on the grass behind the garage when George and I found him.

"Well," I said to Ingham, "how is he this morning?"

"Nervy," said Ingham. "He doesn't like being alone."

As soon as the ape had seen us approaching, he had retired to a slight distance and, squatting down on his haunches, had begun to scratch an armpit.

"Anyone been poking around?" I asked.

"No one but your friend here—and the boss. He was down here early. By the way, if either of you is going to the village I'd be grateful if you'd bring me back some cigarettes. I'm running out of them again and I'm not taking the risk of going to fetch them myself today."

I told him we should be going to the village as soon as George had shown me something he had brought me there to see. "Then I'm going to call on the vicar," I said.

"That isn't a thing I'd do for pleasure," said Ingham.

George was impatient. "D'you reckon Leofric'll do that stunt all over again?" he asked. "Maybe once is enough for him, eh? It must take a good deal of thinkin' out."

"Sure," said Ingham, "and unless he's hungry he won't exert himself."

"But we could try, eh?"

"Sure you can try." He turned to me. "Been giving any thought to that little problem of character I put to you yesterday evening?"

George, who seemed bursting with his own ideas this morning, answered before I could: "That's simple enough, Mr Ingham. You said yourself, didn't you, Leofric's got a likin' for a drive in a car, but Irma was scared of it? Well, whoever did the job must've been watchin' till you set off for the village, then they came down here, got out Mrs Peach's car and tried to put the two chimps into it. Irma was scared and got away and probably went runnin' up to the house to look for Dr Virag, and must've hidden herself somewhere while the search was on. But Leofric settled down to enjoy a nice drive. I suppose there's a road goes somewhere near that wood where you found him?"

"There is," said Ingham, "and I think you've hit it; that's what happened."

"And I suppose you can explain," I said, "why the person chose to come back and stab Irma in a public place like a drawing-room, instead of Leofric, whom he'd taken away with him to a nice secluded wood?"

"You don't need to be sarcastic," said George. "I'm tellin' you, that's what happened."

Ingham nodded. "I never saw anyone come and get the car out of the garage, and yet when it was wanted to go and fetch you from the station, it was standing ready by the gate."

"There you are then," said George to me.

"I thought you'd brought me down here to show me something," I said.

"That's right," said George. "We got to put Leofric back in his cage, and we got to have a banana. It'll interest you, Tobe, it's a wonderful sight. There ain't no trick about it, it's just brains at work."

Ingham called out: "Hi, Leofric!"

They had difficulty in getting Leofric into his cage; he wanted to stay on the hillside. Then, when he was in the cage, with the bolt fastened, they had difficulty in attracting his attention. He squatted down in a corner and went on with his toilet. He scarcely looked at the banana that Ingham held out to him. I suggested that he was obviously not in an obliging mood and that we should get on to the vicarage. But George shook his head. Ingham at last peeled the banana and took a bite off the end, and that had the effect they wanted. Leofric at once started to utter shrill, protesting noises, and seeing Ingham apparently continuing to eat the banana, got up and took a couple of steps towards the front of the cage. Ingham took another bite. Leofric suddenly pounced on a piece of bamboo that was lying on the floor of the cage and waved it furiously at Ingham. His black hair bristled and his savage teeth were bared. Crouching there waving his club he looked incredibly ferocious.

I said: "So they *can* turn vicious."

"Lord, yes," said Ingham, "but when they're vicious they don't bother with sticks, they come straight at you with teeth and claws. This show he's putting on at the moment is just play-acting. Here, Leofric——" He thrust one hand through the bars. Leofric seized it in his mouth, but he did no more than chew at it gently, with his lips drawn over his teeth. Then he stretched one of his own hands through the bars and, gazing at the banana with ardent desire, started to make wheedling noises.

"Now watch," said Ingham.

He put the banana down on the ground about two yards from the cage, and stepped back.

I suppose Leofric had gone through this routine pretty often. Once the problem of reaching the banana must have taken much hard thinking to solve. His attitude to it now was a mixture of petulance and absent-mindedness, as of one who refuses to bring his mind fully to bear upon a tedious, too-familiar difficulty.

First he reached towards the banana with one of his hands. But he checked the movement almost as soon as it had begun, since it was obvious that the banana was a long way beyond his grasp. Then he picked up the bamboo and used it to reach for the fruit. The bamboo, however, was a little under a yard long, and missed the banana by several inches. At that point, looking up at Ingham, Leofric began to complain shrilly.

Ingham replied to him: "No, son, it's your job, not mine."

Leofric stormed a little; then suddenly he went quiet. Turning round, he went to the far corner of the cage again and picked up a second piece of bamboo. He squatted down and clumsily but with great gravity, and with his attention fully concentrated, proceeded to insert the end of one piece of bamboo into the hollow end of the other.

All at once he sprang towards the bars again and, with the lengthened instrument in his hand, triumphantly poked the banana towards him.

George was right; it was a fascinating exhibition.

For the first time I felt some understanding of Virag's absorption in his work.

Suddenly I let out an exclamation: "My God, I see what you mean! It's possible—it's perfectly possible! I see why you said there were no gloves or apron. The bamboo, the knife with the serpent round it, the bloodstains that stopped halfway up. . . ." I clapped George on the shoulder. "I believe you're right. You must be. This explains a whole lot of things."

Ingham drawled ironically: "I reckon Leofric'd be mighty proud if he knew that he'd helped you any. Would you mind explaining to me, then I can pass it on to him when occasion arises."

"We've got to get hold of the knife," I said, "and the bamboo."

"The sergeant took 'em," said George.

"Then we must go and look for the sergeant."

Ingham began again: "Would you mind explaining . . . ?"

I looked into his face and noticed once more the reserve and wariness in the eyes. I said deliberately: "All right, I'll explain. You saw the knife, didn't you, sticking into Irma? You saw the way the blood had splashed over it, just halfway up? Well, at that point there was a projection on the hilt. It was a serpent in relief. Above it the silver was perfectly clean, suggesting that that was where the hand of the killer had covered it. There was a queer thing about it, however. It looked as if the killer had taken only two inches of the hilt into his hand. That's a crazy way to hold a knife. In fact "—I glanced down involuntarily at Ingham's big, muscular hands—"in fact, I doubt if you *could* hold it like that and get any strength behind the blow. I've been puzzling over that ever since I saw it. But now it's clear that what happened was this. There was a piece of bamboo lying in the pool of blood next to Irma. I think the killer held that piece of bamboo, and I think the hilt of the knife was stuck into the piece of bamboo—stuck in as far as the projection made by the serpent. I was wrong in my first assumption —the stabbing wasn't done at close quarters. Whoever did it was standing at least two feet away from Irma. That explains, of course, why he got no blood on his clothes. He stood about two feet off and stabbed her carefully and deliberately, then pulled the bamboo away from the hilt and dropped it on the floor where the blood, gushing out from the wound, would flow over it. That was so that the fact that it was already splashed with blood wouldn't give away how it had been used. And then——"

"That's all we know for the present," said George quickly.

I accepted the caution. "That's right, that's all we know."

Ingham looked at me sardonically, then he turned and stared at Leofric. With one of the pieces of bamboo the keeper started to tap an absent-minded rhythm on the bars of the cage, while Leofric gulped the last shreds of banana.

"Sure," said Ingham softly, "and it's quite a lot too if you come to think of it."

V

Eᴀꜱᴛ Lᴇᴀᴛ ɪɴ the daylight was a pretty place. Its church had a square, solid, age-old dignity, many of the houses were of warm, red, Georgian brick, the pub was a low, white building with a mossy roof and a swinging sign. The village was the sort that would have shown at its best on a picture-postcard.

Yet, even in the daylight, East Leat had a curious eeriness.

That may sound unconvincing. The sunshine was pouring down on to the green, there was the usual coming and going of quiet country folk, there were children taking their dolls out in perambulators, there were the usual cats and dogs and the inevitable ill-adjusted wireless sets droning out through open cottage doors. But all the same there was something dead and decayed about the place.

A cottage, which a short distance away looked neat and cheerful, turned out, when you got closer, to have had several of its windows filled with newspaper instead of with glass. The bright flowers in its garden turned out to be field poppies blazing in unkempt grass. The little girls had greasy, unwashed hair and dirty necks. One of the men lounging near the pub showed, as he turned to stare at us, the bulging eyes and loose, hanging lip of the village idiot.

The police-station opened off a passage between

two buildings. Sergeant Sawbry was not in the least glad to see us. He stood in the doorway and at first refused to discuss the case at all. Fortunately, if he could obstruct our getting in, we could obstruct his getting out, and in about ten minutes he had come to the conclusion that the simplest way to get rid of us and to get home to his dinner was to fetch out the knife and the piece of bamboo and to let us see whether the hilt of the one would fit inside the open end of the other.

They fitted perfectly.

Sawbry thought he saw his opportunity for some fun.

"Now this begins to look like a real interesting case, Mr Dyke," he said. "I see what's in your mind, and I can't say I've heard of such a thing except in a story-book; still, when you've got fancy detectives nosing around a thing you may find out pretty well anything." He leered at me knowingly. "Yes—pretty well anything."

"What are you talking about?" I asked. I had the spear made of the bamboo and the blood-encrusted knife in my hand. I twirled it in the air to see what it felt like. It was an ill-balanced instrument, but on an adversary who was not defending himself it would be quite easy to use.

"What am I talking about?" Sawbry inquired ponderously. "Why, the same as you, aren't I, Mr Dyke? Don't tell me I've misunderstood you!"

"I suppose it's too late to try this thing for fingerprints?" I said.

"It's such a nice fancy idea." Sawbry went on

with his own thoughts dreamily, while his boiled, blue, sarcastic eyes dwelt on my face. " Not the kind of idea a plain man like me'd ever have come on by myself, but, of course, with you to help me . . ."

" What are you talking about, Sergeant? "

" I've been telling you, haven't I, and saying what a nice idea I think it is? " He guffawed. " You just told me, didn't you, the monkey himself went and told you how he did it? The monkey himself! Ha, ha! " He rocked with laughter.

I wondered whether his wife had ever absent-mindedly attempted to roast this piece of beef instead of the Sunday joint. " Ha, ha," I said. I placed the tip of the knife against his blue bosom. " Only Irma wasn't a monkey, Sergeant; she was a chimpanzee, an anthropoid ape, one of your cousins and mine. It's true both apes and monkeys are primates, but then so are lemurs. Have you ever tried calling cousins with a lemur, Sergeant? "

He looked at me suspiciously. " I thought Primate was a word for the Archbishop of Canterbury."

" So it is, Sergeant, so it is—so you see how careful you have to be."

He swelled slightly. " Now let me tell you something, Mr Dyke. My report on this business has gone into Ashingham, and Inspector Port'll be over here this afternoon, and it isn't my business what's to be done next. But all the same I can tell you who killed the animal and why, and it didn't take a lot of fancy detecting to work it out either."

" That's very interesting," I said.

" Oh, I can see you don't believe me," he retorted

jeeringly. "By the time you've finished you'll be proving that Mussolini was over here on the quiet last night and did it himself. But myself, I've got leanings to believing what's in front of my nose."

"And that is?"

He looked at me slyly. I could see the tip of his tongue working round inside his cheek.

I said impatiently: "Come on, George, we're finished here."

"Wait a minute," said Sawbry, "who said I wouldn't tell you? I don't mind saving you a bit of trouble—then you can go back home, can't you, and leave me to get on with my job in peace?"

"Well?"

"Well, it was the keeper," said Sawbry.

I stared at him.

"Ah, you hadn't got there, had you, Mr Dyke? You thought it was Mussolini."

Carefully I laid the knife and bamboo down on the table; it seemed wisest to me in talking to Sawbry not to have a weapon in my hand.

"And how did you arrive at it?" I asked.

"Just put it to myself, *why* did this happen?—that's all."

"And why did it happen?"

He shook his heavy head at me. "I'm afraid it's all too simple for you, Mr Dyke, much too simple."

"Well, why did Ingham stab the chimpanzee?"

"Because his boss told him to, of course."

"Well, well," I said.

I was relieved. It had been a shock to me that this lump of East Leat clay had arrived at the truth as quickly as I had myself. But his present line of thought would not take him far.

"Very interesting indeed," I said with a pleasant smile. "Come along, George, let's go and talk to the vicar."

I thought there were signs of anxiety on Sawbry's face.

"Now, now, Mr Dyke," he said, "don't tell me you've nothing to say about my idea."

I strolled to the doorway.

"And why d'you want to talk to the vicar?" he asked quickly and suspiciously.

"Why not?" I asked.

"But you still haven't said anything about my idea."

I said: "I'm glad you're only calling it an idea now, because ideas can be altered."

"Now look here, Mr Dyke——"

"Why should Dr Virag want his chimpanzee slaughtered?" I asked.

"Because he knew the deal wasn't going through. It's the insurance money he's after now."

"But if Virag had been in such need of cash," I replied, "I've no doubt he could have sold Irma to some other scientific institution. I think he'd have preferred that to killing her. But, as a matter of fact, the deal's already gone through. He's going to get his money."

I was startled by the sudden blaze of disquiet on the sergeant's face. Then I realised that Tom Tadwell of the Cricketers must have brought his troubles to the police as well as to the church.

Chuckling, I patted Sawbry on the shoulder. "So you don't like the idea of local prohibition either. You have my sympathy. But if you go on looking like that I'll start thinking it must have been you that did it, and not Mussolini at all."

His face was red. "How d'you mean—the deal's gone through?"

"Good morning," I replied. "Thanks very much for taking us into your confidence. Now we really must get along to see Mr Teed."

"Gone through!" Sawbry kept at my elbow as I went out into the street, and as I would have started off across the green towards the vicarage, he held me back. Huskily, desperately, he muttered: "Did you say—did you mean—that deal's gone through, Mr Dyke?"

Standing on the pavement, looking across the green, I could see the long, white façade, the mossy roof and swinging sign of the Cricketers.

I might have reassured the sergeant. I might have told him that though the first part of the deal had gone through, there was still a good chance that Lord Nutlin would not betray his faithful adherents. But why trouble to reassure a man who annoyed one so much?

Just then a car went by. It was Kenneth Glynne's, and in it, beside the doctor, sat Marion Teed.

Sawbry's excitement suddenly transferred itself to another object. "There now, it looks as if it's true then!" he exclaimed. "Miss Teed and the doctor —did you see? I'd heard tell they were getting married, but that's the first time I've ever seen them around together. When my missus told me about it I didn't believe it. 'No,' I said, 'it's on account of the other one he's always up at Miss Miall's.' Seems I may have been wrong. Well, if I was, I'll be mighty glad, because he's a rare good fellow, is the doctor; he's always ready to take all the trouble in the world. Only last night he was up till five o'clock with Jessie Warrell. She was bad too—it's her first, though she and Ted have been married this seven year. Reckon the doctor's feeling pretty tired this morning. Well, he'll do better with Miss Teed as a wife than he would've with the other one."

" The other one? " I asked innocently.

He snorted. " Let me tell you," he said, " I don't hold with these new-fangled ways of divorce and all. A woman takes her husband for better or worse, even if he does turn out to be a waster like Peach. That's the way I look at it. Still, if she does go and have the law on him, then she ought to live quiet and not start rolling her eyes at every man she meets —anyway, not until the whole business is done with, legal and proper. And what I say is, if Kitty Garner had remained in her own station of life, instead of getting grand notions all along of being adopted by Miss Miall, then she wouldn't be divorcing any husband now, she'd be putting up with him, the same as poor Polly did with Gus Garner. But they're a bad lot, those Garners, all of them. It was because of the way Gus Garner and Polly neglected the child that Miss Miall adopted her. And when Kitty was older, did she ever give any help to her own people? Not she. Miss Miall helped Polly Garner more than

155

once—poor Polly never had much of a chance with a drunken, thieving husband like that, and being a little soft in the head besides—but Kitty always turned up her nose at them. She went dreaming around the place with that angel's face of hers, looking as refined as you please and carrying on with all the young men in the neighbourhood. And then she went and married Peach. But that was a mistake on her part, mind you, because when that happened Miss Miall cut her loose and told her she wasn't wanted around at 2 Titmore Lane. It's only about six months past that she worms herself in again with stories of how badly her husband's treating her, and how she don't want anything but to come home and comfort Miss Miall's old age. I reckon she found Peach hadn't as much money as she wanted. I said to my wife, I said: 'You'll see,' I said, ' she'll be up to her games again in no time. But she'd better be careful,' I said, 'because Miss Miall'd never stand for anything wrong.' Sure enough, in a little while the doctor's off up to Miss Miall's every other day, and——"

"Yes, but it seems to be Miss Teed he's marrying."

It stemmed the flow. The sergeant looked rather bewildered.

"Yes," he said, " yes—to be sure, Miss Teed."

As George and I set off across the green towards the vicarage, Sawbry remained standing on the pavement, chewing on the fact, which he seemed to find reassuring though still somewhat unconvincing, that the doctor was marrying Marion Teed.

*   *   *   *   *

I myself found the engagement difficult to fit into the scheme of things. It was not even as if it were of long standing, with Katharine Peach and her destructive beauty a new, unforeseen element in the situation. Katharine Peach had told me that Glynne and Marion had been engaged for a week.

It was as I was reflecting that before now men have got married in the hope of cutting themselves loose from a profitless passion, that I noticed Glynne's car drawn up in front of a row of cottages near the church. Marion Teed was sitting in it alone.

She beckoned to us.

" Kenneth's gone in to see how Jessie Warrell and her baby are," she said, " then we're—we're going to wire Lord Nutlin. We've decided Miss Miall ought to know about what happened to Irma."

" You're quite right," I said, " she ought."

" It'd have been better if we could have got everything solved first, but . . ." She shrugged. She sat twisting a small gold ring on her finger.

" You're sure Miss Miall's with Lord Nutlin? " I asked.

" Yes, I think so," she said.

" You mean she's staying with him? "

" Oh no, I shouldn't think she's doing that. But she went to see him to—well, to argue with him."

" In other words, your uncle was right when he said there'd been a mistake," I said. " Miss Miall thought Lord Nutlin was serious, and Lord Nutlin thought Miss Miall wasn't."

" Oh, you mustn't laugh at her," she said quickly; " it isn't nearly as fantastic as it sounds. Even if you don't share Miss Miall's views on drink, you'd agree that the amount of drunkenness in this village is perfectly appalling. It's the isolation, you see, the lack of other amusements, and, I suppose, just a sort of habit people have got into. Miss Miall's methods may be bizarre, but her ends generally have a good deal of sound sense about them. And she didn't mean simply to get the public house closed; she was going to open some other places of entertainment." She eyed me to see how I was responding. But as I found nothing to say she looked away dispiritedly. "Oh, well," she said, "it doesn't matter what you think, since it was a mistake, anyway."

"By the way," I said, "when did you find out it was a mistake?"

"When Lord Nutlin wired," she replied. "Miss Miall wrote to him as soon as she heard Dr Virag had arrived in London with the chimpanzees. Lord Nutlin wired back that the whole thing was a mistake and he'd never dreamt that she'd taken him seriously."

"And so Miss Miall descended on him in person?"

"You see," she said gravely, "all sorts of people do things if Miss Miall actually goes to see them who wouldn't if she simply wrote them a letter."

"She's stayed arguing with him a long time," I said.

"Yes, and I think that must mean she's hopeful she can make him change his mind. That's why I think I ought to try and get in touch with her and tell her what's happened. I'm afraid it'll be a terrible blow. But it's better to tell her than to let her persuade him and then find out that now it's she herself who can't fulfil her side of the bargain." She glanced round towards the Warrells' cottage. "I wish Kenneth would hurry up. He's going to drive me into Ashingham, because anything one wires or says on the telephone in this village becomes public property. I'm afraid it means lunch will be late, as I shouldn't think we'd get home before half-past one. Have you been seeing Sawbry?"

"Yes, he says he's sent his report of the case in to Ashingham."

"Of course, he doesn't want to catch whoever did it," she said. "I expect everyone in the village is delighted about it. I've been wondering—don't you think it might have been someone from the village, Mr Dyke? It's just the sort of brutal, stupid thing some of these people might do. Don't you think so?"

"No, Miss Teed, I don't."

"But why not?" She was nervously twisting the ring on her finger. "It seems to me much the most probable explanation."

"You see," I said, "the weapon used was a rather unusual one. It consisted of a knife, which was kept in a cabinet in the sitting-room, and a piece of bamboo. The hilt of the knife was stuck into the open end of the bamboo so that the killer could stand a couple of feet off and be safe from the spurting blood. Now it seems to me that whoever thought of that weapon had seen something like it before—had seen, that's to say, Leofric or Irma sticking pieces of bamboo together to reach for bananas. But I don't think any of the East Leat citizenry have had that opportunity."

She looked at me dully, then again she glanced impatiently at the cottage door.

"I do wish Kenneth would hurry," she said, "it's going to make lunch so dreadfully late if we don't get started soon."

"I shouldn't worry about that. Why not take a day off and have lunch in Ashingham? We'll look after ourselves this end."

"Oh, I couldn't do that," she said with disapproval.

"It's what I'd do if I were you," I said. "And then I'd go to the pictures. However, if the suggestion doesn't appeal to you, would you mind answering one more question? Is it true, Miss Teed, that Miss Miall considers Dr Virag has earned his money for the experimental station at Tobago?"

"Of course," she said.

"You mean she intends to let him have the money irrespective of how unamenable Lord Nutlin turns out to be?"

"Naturally," she said; "Miss Miall is always the soul of——"

"Ah yes—the soul of fairness. Good. Well, thanks, Miss Teed. George and I are just about to pay a visit to the vicar. We'll see you at lunch— unless you change your mind and decide to take a day off in Ashingham."

Leaving her protesting that with so many guests and with so much to do the idea was unthinkable,

George and I continued on our way to the vicarage.

The house which I had noticed the evening before as a great ghostly shell of a building, standing in a garden which was divided from the churchyard by a low yew hedge, was one of those vicarages that reduce the incumbent to bankruptcy. In the days when parsons had ten or eleven children it would have housed them all. Built of soiled-looking brick, it had gables and a turret or two, and in the state of decay it had reached, had an air of pompous squalor.

The house paid no attention to us when I rang the bell. As I took my hand away from the ancient bell-pull it stayed hanging out of its socket instead of springing back into place. The sound of the bell pealing through the house died away. There was no responsive sound of footsteps within.

George, who had been growing increasingly moody all the morning, muttered: " Are you sure he lives here? "

At a glance I should certainly have taken the house to be uninhabited. The curtainless windows stared blindly, the garden was a tangle of ramblers that had not been pruned for years, one of the stone balls that crowned the pretentious gateposts had been broken off. The green paint on the woodwork had faded to a pale mildew colour and, cracked and peeling, helped to produce the unpleasant look of corruption.

After a minute or so I tried the bell again, but the bell-pull only drooped brokenly.

As I began on the knocker some children at the gate started calling out to us, but I could make nothing of what they said; the local accent made them all sound as if they had cleft palates.

"I *think*," said George, scratching his head, "they're tellin' us to go round to the side door."

"Well, we'll try it," I said.

Making our way along a paved path that skirted the house, we discovered that the vicar lived in a few rooms at the back of the gaunt building. Curtains at the windows showed us which rooms were inhabited, curtains of almost as faded and dreary a green as the paint on the window-frames. Through one of these windows I saw that the room inside was a kitchen; it was large and dark, with a high dresser and a massive range, but with bookcases, a rocking-chair and a writing-table to show that it was used as a sitting-room.

I remarked: "Teed doesn't seem to spend much of his income on his living-quarters."

I gripped the knocker on the back door. It clattered noisily, and after a moment I heard the slithering and slapping of loose slippers on the tiles within.

As the door opened, Teed, in a thick, frowsy dressing-gown, yawned in our faces.

He said: "Pardon me.... I had a vague thought I heard the bell a few minutes ago, but no one ever goes to the front door, so I dismissed it.... I'm so glad you found your way.... Come in, come in."

Still yawning, he turned, and we followed him into the kitchen.

Wrapping his dressing-gown carefully around him, he lowered his huge, bulgy body into the rocking-chair and waved us to a couple of kitchen-chairs.

"Hope you'll excuse me," he went on as he set

himself a-rocking. "I've only just staggered out of bed. I'd rather a bad night, engrossed with too many disturbing thoughts, and this morning didn't feel at all well. I'm not at all in good health, you know. That's why people put up with my ways, I suppose; they know I shan't last long. Now what can I do for you? Delighted to help in any way I can. Always delighted, always, to help our dear Rosa Miall."

I brought out my cigarettes, the vicar took one and we sat puffing smoke on to the stale air of the kitchen for a moment before I answered.

Then I went straight to the point. "Look here, vicar, what is it you've got on Christopher Ingham?"

The pale eyebrows on the big, yellow face waggled up and down for a moment as if the man was startled. For an instant he put a brake on his rocking.

"Christopher Ingham?" he said. "Ah yes, the keeper."

"You recognised him yesterday," I said. "When he denied it you let it pass. But you recognised him all right."

"I see you're a very acute observer, Mr Dyke," said Teed, smiling a little.

"It didn't need anything particularly acute in the way of observation to see that," I said.

"Ah, don't deny it!" There was the touch of giggling coquetry in his tone which I had already found peculiarly offensive. "All yesterday evening I was watching you. I've never felt myself to be under such keen observation. I knew you were noting down in your memory every little movement any of

163

us made and every little word we spoke. I'm sure Dr Virag is most fortunate in having obtained your services."

"Thanks very much. Put it in writing and I'll add it to my testimonials." I tipped my chair back and unthinkingly set it swaying in time with Teed's. "Who and what, Mr Teed, is Christopher Ingham?"

An expression of gravity slid across the yellow expanse of face.

"Dear me, I wish this hadn't happened," said Teed. "You're putting me in a very awkward position."

I was glad to hear it, though I had not expected him to start admitting it at this stage.

"You see," he went on, "I feel that one owes it to the poor fellow not to——" He hesitated, looking at me with his head on one side and his mouth puckered up into a small, dubious pout.

"I've no intention of using his past against him," I said sardonically, "if that's what you're afraid of."

He gave a superficial smile. "Ah, I'm glad you said that. It does make things easier. Knowledge of others is always a responsibility. Partly, it was thinking over that poor man's sad case that kept me awake so long last night. In a way I felt I owed it to Dr Virag to make sure he understands just what kind of character he's employing, but at the same time I couldn't help feeling that——" He made a fluttering gesture with one hand. "After all, it isn't for me to judge others, but only to help them, when I can, to judgment of themselves. Don't you agree with me?"

"All I want to know is Ingham's real name and

the circumstances that made him change it," I said.

"Just so. And your motives in trying to make me disclose this information are no doubt admirable, but that doesn't help to solve the problem that hangs on my conscience. A man's future may be in my hands. Shall I fling it out on to the public highway, where anyone who passes can trample it underfoot, or——"

"Mr Teed, let me assure you that if you don't want to help me I can set other inquiries going to get the information I need," I said. "There are always ways of getting this kind of information if one takes the trouble. It'll take longer and it may stir up unnecessary mud; for all I know, it may bring actual distress to people of whom at the moment I know nothing, since a man's secret is very seldom his exclusive property. But I'll get the information in the end."

"Oh dear, I know it, I know it."

The vicar closed his eyes. As the heavy body rocked gently backwards and forwards I saw that his lips were moving slightly. It looked as if he were praying for divine guidance. After a moment he opened his eyes.

"Does the name Charles Illstree mean anything to you?" he asked abruptly.

I jerked forward in my chair.

Charles Illstree!

That name immediately set a clangour of associations going in my head; it called up visions of newspaper headlines and smudged photographs, memories of angry discussions in pubs and railway trains; it took hold of my mind like a familiar tune. Yet it was a moment before I had pulled into shape the recollections startled into being by Teed's sudden question.

I suppose I looked blank for an instant.

Teed went on: " Charles Illstree was the man who was tried at Ashingham six years ago for the murder of Minnie Kirtin in one of the hotels there. Surely you remember it? "

" He was acquitted," I said.

" Yes—because in English law there's no such thing as a verdict of Not Proven. There was no evidence to prove that his story of the girl being shot during a struggle in which he was trying to take the revolver away from her was not the truth. Yet everyone—everyone but the judge and jury— was certain that he was guilty. I remember I found it very strange. I was quite startled by the blood-lust to which the rustic can be roused. However, I believe it was more or less the same all over the country. When Illstree was acquitted there were dark murmurings about one law for the rich and another for the poor—peculiarly senseless murmurings in this particular case, because though Illstree came of good family he was practically penniless. What little money he had, he had been burning up with the girl. Myself, I never felt clear about the case. He called the police to the dead girl so promptly, he seemed so frank, that one would have felt inclined to agree with the verdict wholeheartedly except that so many circumstances were against him." Teed stopped and stared up at the discoloured ceiling. "However, it's not for me to doubt that verdict. The poor man must have suffered much since then, whether he was innocent or guilty."

"You saw him at the trial then?"

"No, I don't frequent murder trials, Mr Dyke. But I saw him immediately after he'd been released. People were standing still in the street to stare at him as he walked along, and I heard a man call out: 'There's Illstree!' There was none of the enthusiasm there usually is over an acquittal. At first people just stared at him, then they started to shout foul names at him. I realised then, looking into his face as he passed me, that the public certainty of his guilt would follow him almost as relentlessly as if the verdict of 'innocent' had never been passed. I remember feeling overcome by an immense pity for him."

"Well," I said, "thank you for telling me."

Leaning forward, Teed put a thick hand on my arm.

"Mr Dyke, I've told you this believing in your understanding and discretion. Remember, he was acquitted. None of us has any right to question his innocence of the crime of murder. Plainly he changed his name and sank to his present kind of employment because the filth of that trial stuck to him. I'm glad he appears to be secure and reasonably content. Think well, I beg you, before you do anything that may plunge him back into shame and suffering."

While he had been speaking, most of Teed's unpleasant mannerisms had dropped away. He was speaking simply and earnestly. It would have been easy just then to let myself believe that all that was really wrong with the man was his ponderous, ugly body and his unlovely features, that most of his giggling and coyness and slyness came from self-consciousness about his huge unattractiveness, and that for all unfortunates, whether they were sinned against or sinning, he had a heart full of sympathy and kindness.

My momentary response to this apparent change in him, however, left me with an even sharper sense of repulsion than usual.

"I told you, I've no intention of using his past against him—whatever others may do." I managed, by tipping my chair back again, to slide my arm out of his grasp without actually shaking him off. "But tell me, apart from the question of his past, don't you believe it was Charles Illstree who stabbed Irma?"

The vicar shook with gusty laughter. "That's a swift descent from the sublime to the ridiculous, isn't it? Somehow it brings the thought of a drink into my mind. What about it?"

Heaving himself on to his feet he lumbered across to a cupboard and brought out a bottle and glasses. It was some minutes before I could get him back to the question of Ingham and the chimpanzees, because he refused to take it as anything but a joke.

"Not that I don't feel proper pity for the poor animal, and disgust at the manner of its death," he said presently, as with a glass in his hand he settled himself in the rocking-chair again and arranged the

168

folds of his dressing-gown over his knees. " But my own view, if you want to know it, is that the stabbing was done in self-defence. To me that seems the only reasonable solution. Any other explanation is too fantastic. Perhaps it was Ingham who did it—on that I've no opinion. To tell the truth, I'm not particularly interested in the matter. I see your friend doesn't look particularly interested either." He turned to smile at George, who had been listening in broody silence, and who was now staring into the glass Teed had given him, gently tipping it this way and that so that the liquid inside it was set spinning.

I said: " George is generally a good deal more interested than he appears. And I don't think you need try to convince me that you aren't interested in what Miss Miall intended to do with the chimpanzees."

" Ah, I *was* interested in that," said the vicar. " I certainly was. But my interest waned when I learnt the village wasn't in any danger. You see, as soon as Tom Tadwell came rushing in here with his extraordinary story and the letter Miss Miall had written him—I wish I had that letter to show you; it was a most remarkable effusion, quite in Miss Miall's best vein—I decided to get in touch with Lord Nutlin and find out if there was any substance in Miss Miall's claims. Perhaps you think that as a clergyman I ought to have supported her. Believe me "
—he sipped some of his whisky—" I'm not lacking in admiration for the lovely virtue of temperance; also I deplore the rather excessive amount of drunkenness that certainly occurs in this village. But

still it seems to me that to deprive poor people of one of their only pleasures is a strange way of encouraging godliness. I fear that it would probably lead only to their adopting even more dubious forms of entertainment—for instance, football pools or politics. So, as I was saying, I decided to get in touch with Lord Nutlin. He seemed greatly amused and I had it from him that East Leat has nothing to fear. For me that was an end of the matter. I'm afraid I went on feeling angry and uncharitable about it for some time, but I'm glad to say I've recovered my sense of humour. That's what one needs all the time when one's dealing with Miss Miall, you know—a sense of humour. Poor, dear Miss Miall."

I was watching the small, bloodshot eyes very carefully.

"You mean that you knew Miss Miall's scheme had flopped some time before the chimpanzee was killed?"

"I knew it the day before yesterday," he answered.

"I wonder if you could prove that, Mr Teed."

I said it casually; I was fumbling with a packet of cigarettes as I spoke. But I was ready to notice the slightest change on his moon of a countenance.

What I noticed was a sudden, complete stillness.

Then, after a moment, the yellow face smiled at me.

"Of course I quite understand the implications of that question, Mr Dyke."

"Good," I said, "that saves trouble."

He gave his little giggle. "If you were a policeman I should now insist on your warning me that anything I said might be taken down and used in evidence."

"If I were a policeman I should no doubt oblige."

"Ha, ha!" He gulped down his whisky and reached out a hand for the bottle. "So you think that in my righteous wrath at the puritanical tyranny of Miss Miall, I used my knowledge of poor Charles Illstree's past to force him to slaughter a chimpanzee to which he was no doubt much attached, and to betray an employer he no doubt deeply respects? You believe that?"

I replied: "I only asked you a question."

"You've asked a great many questions, and that's the thought behind them."

"It'd be easy enough for you to disprove," I said, "by showing that at the time the chimpanzee was killed you already knew the village wasn't in danger."

"Ah, if I could produce a letter, for instance."

"Exactly."

"I'm afraid that Lord Nutlin and I communicated by telephone."

"That's a pity," I said.

He tittered. "Mr Dyke, please tell me, are you serious in this accusation?"

"To tell the truth, there's a certain lack of seriousness—at any rate, there's an overdose of the bizarre and the ridiculous—about everything connected with this case," I said. "It makes it difficult to keep a sense of proportion. But I'm relatively serious. If I find I'm quite wrong I'll apologise. But I'm going to the trouble of checking that call of yours. Did you telephone from here?"

"Ah no, nor from the village either. One doesn't telephone from East Leat about anything at all private; one goes to Ashingham."

"I was afraid so. Then the only thing to do is to ring up Lord Nutlin."

He nodded. "Do—it will set my mind at rest. Dear me, this is all very intriguing. I wonder what there is about me that's made you leap to this astonishing conclusion. I'm used to considering myself a rather unsatisfactory individual, but never realised I might be suspected of a crime like blackmail."

"If you remember," I said, "the first time I saw you, you were shaking your fist at some empty cages."

"So I was," he murmured, "so I was." He drew his breath in slowly. "Quite deplorable, I agree with you. But my time here in East Leat, a time that should have been a struggle, a worthy struggle, with ignorance, vice and unhappiness, has in fact been one long, ceaseless struggle with Miss Miall, with her passion for domination and her eccentricities. You caught me in a moment of weakness, expressing a great deal of bottled-up resentment against the good lady. I regret it intensely; it was vindictive and unchristian of me. But I assure you, I have no antagonism to chimpanzees as such—nor even to those two particular chimpanzees."

I got to my feet.

"Your niece and Dr Glynne are just going into Ashingham to do some telephoning," I said. "Unless they've already gone I'll ask them to take me."

"Good," said the vicar, "good."

George also got to his feet. But clearing his throat and fidgeting with his feet on the rug, he chose that moment to address the vicar.

"Excuse me, Mr Teed," he said, "but would you mind if I was to put a question too."

The vicar turned a smiling look on him. "By all means—go ahead." Then as George remained tongue-tied and embarrassed, he repeated graciously, "Go ahead—ask anything."

Drawing intersecting arcs on the floor with the toe of one shoe, George said: "You was sittin' by the roadside quite a while, wasn't you, Mr Teed—I mean, you was sittin' there long enough to smoke three cigarettes?"

"I believe I was. There's a very nice view from that spot," said the vicar.

"That's right—you can see the wood from there, can't you?"

"Yes, and a beautiful wood it is too—nothing but great, noble, old beech trees."

"That's right. Then maybe you saw Mr Ingham comin' back from the wood, bringin' the other chimpanzee, the one what didn't get hurt, along with him?"

"As a matter of fact, I did," said Teed. "But I doubt if Mr Dyke will believe me. He'll think the evidence a little too convenient."

George cleared his throat again. "Did you see anyone else while you was sittin' there?"

"Returning from the wood?"

"From anywhere. Or goin' anywhere. Did you

see anyone else at all while you was sittin' by the road? "

" I saw Mrs Peach returning from the village with a package which later turned out to have contained the whisky that appeared at supper. And I saw Dr Glynne drive down the hill."

" That was when he was going for the police," I said.

" And you didn't see nobody else? " asked George.

" Nobody."

" You're dead certain sure? " George insisted.

" Absolutely."

" Thanks, Mr Teed."

With a deep frown marking his smooth, pink forehead, George followed me to the door.

The vicar shuffled after us to show us out.

As we were going down the paved path that skirted the house, and out once more on to the sunlit green where the little girls with cleft palates were still playing with the battered dolls in their toy-perambulators, I heard George muttering to himself.

I turned on him with irritation: " You've gone damned thoughtful all of a sudden. What the hell's the matter? "

" Nothin' ain't the matter," he answered woodenly. But he stood still and stared at me with wide-open, troubled eyes. Suddenly, for some reason, I was reminded of the mood in which I myself had stood here yesterday evening. " No—nothin' ain't the matter," said George. " It's just that I reckon I know who done it. And I got a feelin' . . . I got a feelin'

I know *why* it was done, Tobe.... And it's mighty nasty."

* * * * *

At that moment Glynne came out of the cottage. We met beside the car. But it was empty.

Glynne said: "Hullo—have you seen Marion?"

His eyes looked heavy with lack of sleep and there were haggard lines on his face.

"She was waiting here in the car when we saw her last," I said.

Glynne's hand went clawing through his hair. "I wonder where she's got to. I was going to drive her into Ashingham to do some telephoning. We thought we ought to try and get in touch with Miss Miall. Marion said she'd wait here, and I did my best to be quick, but I couldn't get away from Ted Warrell. It wasn't the baby he wanted to talk about, it was cricket. I suppose you haven't seen Marion?" He had already forgotten that he had asked the question. His voice had the thin, uneven quality that goes with tiredness and bad nerves.

I repeated what I had said to him.

"I suppose she must have gone home," he said peevishly. "She said she'd wait and I was as quick as I could be, but damn it all, I can't start scamping my job just because she wants to telephone and for some reason won't use a local call-box."

I said: "She seemed to have it rather on her mind that through her going to Ashingham our lunch was going to be late. Perhaps she decided not to go till the afternoon."

175

"There you are"—and he swore—"that's Marion! I don't believe she has a single thought that isn't somehow tangled up with housekeeping. There's something all wrong about it. It's morbid. It's got nothing to do with making a house a comfortable and homely place to live in. There's no real consideration for other people in it. She uses her work as a whip to lash herself with; it's self-laceration. She's the kind of person who'd try getting up to dust the china when she'd got pneumonia." He tugged open the door of the car.

It seemed to me a strange way to speak of the girl he was going to marry.

Looking round at me he went on: "Can I drop you anywhere? I'd better go up to the house, I suppose, and see if that's where she's gone."

"Thanks," I said.

When we had got into the car he let the clutch in so that the car lurched violently, and he swore again.

"I shan't be sorry if I don't have to drive into Ashingham," he said. "My God, I'm tired!"

"I want to go to Ashingham myself," I said. "Like Miss Teed, I want to telephone and don't want to take the whole of East Leat into my confidence. You know, I've never realised before how complicated simple village life seems to be. Perhaps, if I can borrow Mrs Peach's car, I could take Miss Teed and save you the drive."

"I'd be damned grateful if you would," he said immediately.

"How far is it?"

"About eighteen miles. The only thing is——"

He broke off and chewed on his lower lip, then swore at a van that was backing across the road; his brakes went on so that the whole car shuddered. " No, I'd better take her myself. If I don't she'll think I got out of it because I didn't want to take her or something. I don't know if you've ever had much to do with a girl like that. She's a mass of the grimmest sort of repressions. None of her emotions function naturally and freely. Either they're squashed altogether or they get out of hand and burst out in a thoroughly distorted, hysterical form."

It struck me again that I had never heard a man talk in quite that way about a girl with whom he claimed to be in love. Probably if he had not spent the night wrestling for the life of Jessie Warrell and her child Glynne would never have given himself away so badly.

As we waited for the van to get out of the way, I started working out the way it must have happened. Glynne, fighting with his desire for a woman whom he himself in his calm moments knew to be stupid, egotistical and possibly depraved— " rotten right through," as Katharine Peach had said to me in her vague, smiling way—had clutched for support at what he had taken to be the strength and integrity of the quiet girl in the background. By now he knew his mistake. That apparent calm was simply the frozen shell that held in an explosive force of distorted emotion. Moreover, Marion knew why he wanted to marry her. Because she was in love with him, she was desperately trying to keep her hold on him. But in her jealousy and humiliation, she never gave him a chance to enjoy a moment's closeness or security with her.

At that point I thought once more how remarkable it was that in the situation which I had been gradually coming to understand, it was a chimpanzee that had been murdered. . . .

" What the ruddy hell does he think he's doing? " burst viciously from Glynne as the van went on zigzagging about the road; then, seizing an instant when the van was over to one side, Glynne, blaring wildly on his horn, sent his car leaping forward, and with only a slight crashing against his back bumper as he scraped past, tore on up Titmore Lane.

" I suppose you haven't got anywhere yet with that business last night," he said.

" You mean the croaking of the chimp? Well, yes and no. We've managed to put certain things together—and found how nicely they fit inside one another."

" Are you talking about real discoveries," he asked, " or merely suspicions? "

" Some of each," I said.

" It's a nightmare business," he said. " I don't suppose it affects you in the same way as it does me—you aren't closely connected with any of the people. But I keep wondering which of them, which person I know . . . I don't mean I'm sentimentalising about the chimp, and if it looked like an ordinary killing of fear or rage it'd never have got on my nerves in the way it has. It's the insanity in it that's getting me down. There's some beastly twist in somebody's mind. . . ." He glanced round at

178

me. " Still, it could have been somebody from the village, couldn't it? I should think there are plenty of people there who'd be glad of a chance to get back at Miss Miall for some of her little bits of interference. Marion thinks it must be someone from the village."

I gave him the same reason as I had given the girl why I did not agree.

As I finished describing the weapon the killer had used Glynne said: " That sounds rather ingenious. I should think you're right—it doesn't sound like the kind of thing that'd come into the head of the average villager. And that means that somebody's brain——" He stopped. There was a haunted look in his eyes. I thought I could guess pretty easily what the suspicions were that were troubling him.

George, who was sitting in the back of the car, leant forward and said in Glynne's ear: " Say, doctor, would you mind just stoppin' the car? I'd like to get out."

I looked round. " What d'you want to get out for? "

" Stretch me legs," said George.

" You stretched them all the way down to the village."

" That's right—but I'd like to stretch them some more."

His eyes met mine with some sort of a message in them. I had no idea what it was, but I said no more. Glynne had stopped the car. George skipped out and said: " Thanks." The car went on.

"Anyway," Glynne growled, shifting uneasily in his seat, "I'm fed up with it all—with chimps, with babies that turn up at three in the morning, with hysterical people, with everything—my God, I'm fed up."

I said: "It seems a suitable moment, if that's so, to press your advantage with Virag."

"What d'you mean?"

"Wasn't he saying that you ought to be doing his sort of work instead of your own?"

He turned on me. He looked immensely startled.

"You see," I said, "you came and discussed it all with Miss Teed outside my bedroom window last night."

"Oh. . . ." A dozen questions leapt at me out of his over-bright eyes. Then he turned away his head. He said dully, without antagonism: "So you listened, did you?"

"That's my job."

"How true. Stupid of me—I ought to have remembered the room'd be occupied. We often sit there. Then you know about Marion and me being engaged. But I expect you'd know that anyway—everyone knows." He suddenly laughed. "But you needn't think that Marion killed Irma out of jealousy —I mean because of my wanting to go to Tobago. Did you think that?"

"Naturally I've considered it along with the other possibilities," I said.

"For one thing," he said, "I don't suppose Virag was serious. I'll stay in this damned hole for the rest of my life or until I——" His head jerked up. "What's happening?"

We had just swung round the bend in the road.

There was the white-painted gate about twenty yards farther on; there was Mrs Peach's cream-coloured saloon in the road; and there were Marti Virag, Ingham and Leofric in the car. Dr Virag himself was just getting into it. The car was piled up with luggage.

As Glynne pulled up I jumped out and went running round to the other car.

I had arrived just in time to stop Dr Virag setting off for America.

VI

I GOT VIRAG into the drawing-room.

" Now what's all this? " I asked.

Looking a little sheepish, Paul Virag crossed the room. His heavy walk had the awkwardness of embarrassment; he held his short arms away from his sides as if he needed them to balance with. Sitting down on one of the oak settles he began to knead his knees.

" It is no use, Mr Dyke—I go. I pay you your fee, but I go."

" To America? "

" Yes, to America. Home first, but then to America. I am sorry I waste your time. There is a train for London this afternoon, so we go by that train. I leave you a cheque. You tell me what sum I shall write on it."

" But look here, if you go now and take Leofric with you, you'll muck everything properly."

" I shall what, please? "

" You'll completely ruin your chances of keeping on your experimental station."

" They are a ruin already."

" They are not—and you know it."

He went on kneading his knees. There was a half-dreamy look in the fine blue eyes under the level brows.

"No," he said after a moment, "I know what you are thinking. You are thinking that I may have that money if I want it. That is quite true. I know no reason to think Miss Miall is a lady without honour; the day I arrive she say to me I shall have the money now that she have the chimpanzees. But that is not the whole of the matter."

"Why isn't it?"

He clicked his tongue impatiently. "Mr Dyke, as I bring you here for nothing, as I waste your time, as I am not at all satisfactory in the way I give you employment, I am most anxious, please, not to give offence. But now whether I go or stay, whether I take that money or not, it is my own business—no?"

"Yes, Dr Virag. All the same, if you don't take that money people may think——"

He gave his very agreeable smile. "If I do not take the money it is permissible to say there may be one hundred and seventeen different reasons why I will not take it."

"Quite true—but there's only one of the hundred and seventeen that recommends itself to the ordinary person."

He shrugged. "Never am I taking much notice of the ordinary person."

"But in heaven's name," I said, "why act as if you accepted responsibility for the killing?—because that's the interpretation that's bound to be put on it if you go now."

His gaze, in which there was the strange mixture of acuteness and innocence which is seldom to be seen except on the faces of men of the highest intelligence, met my look with quiet humour.

"For your sake indeed I should like to remain," he said. "I find you personally most interesting."

"But don't you see——"

"Yes, yes, of course I see. I see everything, Mr Dyke. And I make up my mind to go away."

"Don't you see that if you wait until Miss Miall gets back," I said, "and then perhaps make her the offer of another chimpanzee to replace Irma——?"

He leapt to his feet.

"Another?" he bawled at me. "Did you say *another*?"

"Your daughter told me you had fifteen or sixteen more."

His face grew dark. "I am not giving another, I wish I am never giving any at all, to this old, mad woman. I have serious purposes with my animals, they are not for use in a harlequinade. I go and I take Leofric away with me. I have enough of all this farce. If she say I do not keep my promise I will send her a pink elephant or a rattlesnake to give to her beer-manufacturer, but my valuable and intelligent chimpanzees I prefer shall be treated with respect. Yes, I do not even leave her Leofric. I am made up in my mind. I go."

"To America?"

The passion went out of his voice. He said equally: "I shall like it very much in America. I am reluctant to go only that to be a professor is much

work, much distraction. There are students every-
where, there are lectures to give, there are other professors with whom to make intrigues and arguments,
there are professors' wives with whom not to make
intrigues, there are dinner-parties, there is organis-
ing. It is a very beautiful life and most necessary to
our high, scientific civilisation. But I am happier
alone with my chimpanzees and one or two assistants.
Like so I am doing a great deal more work. But still,
it is better I go. Better," he added thoughtfully,
" for everyone."

" I suppose you've a definite offer of a job—I mean
a chair—somewhere? " I said. " You aren't just
going on spec? "

" Naturally I have definite offer," he said. " I have
definite offer also to go to Russia—in fact, I am
promised a bathroom if I go to Russia. In America
they make no mention of any bathroom, but if I go
to Russia I cannot take my chimpanzees because of
the climate and so I have to begin new work on rats
or dogs, which are not so interesting to me. So I go
to America."

It seemed to me there was nothing more I could
say.

I felt pretty sure he had made up his mind that
Ingham had killed Irma. But since Ingham was in
his employment, Virag had evidently decided to
accept responsibility for the killing himself.

I said with a shrug: " Well, that's that then."

Virag stood up and held out his hand. " Believe
me, Mr Dyke, I am grateful. You are working very
hard in my interest. To please you I would like to

185

remain. If it were only of myself I have to think I stay and wait till you have found out everything. But I am already thinking of myself too much. I have fulfilled my duties as scientist at the expense of other duties. My daughter will be happier in America."

"There you're quite right," I said.

"You see how it is with her," he said. "My wife die many years ago. I know very little of children; always I am doing my best, I see she has good nurses to take care of her health, I see nobody teaches her a lot of nonsense of all kinds—but still I do not understand her, I make mistakes. Here in Europe, travelling about with her, I begin to see what mistakes I have made. She has been too much alone; it has made her nervous, selfish and unsure of herself. She lives in a world of fantasy, in which I am the ogre and every new man she meets is the Prince Charming. Every new assistant who come to me in Tobago she falls in love with. She has once fallen in love with Ingham. Now it is Dr Glynne. Tomorrow perhaps —if we do not go away—it is you! Then one day perhaps she meet a man who will take advantage of it, and then I am afraid she will have great unhappiness, for she has no detachment, no self-control and no understanding of herself. And always she will be afraid to come to me with her troubles."

"But couldn't you send her off on her own to a university or an art-school or something?" I suggested.

He shook his head. "The money I ask for from Miss Miall is enough for my work and enough so I can live, but I have not felt I have the right to ask for a big income for myself. I could not pay for her journeys and her fees and all the rest. But with the salary of a professor I shall be very well off, and so shall Marti." He smiled. "It is very sensible of me. Never in my life am I very sensible, but now—now I see it is necessary."

"Well, it's your own affair," I admitted.

"I tell you, if it was only of myself I have to think . . . But also I must think of Ingham. For his sake too it is better if we go."

"Ingham?" I said quickly.

Virag moved to the window and looked out.

"I tell you this in confidence, Mr Dyke. Ingham is a man who has suffered great misfortunes. He is a good, reliable man, but life has been unkind to him. Particularly it has been unkind to him here in this very district. He has been very unwilling to come; only because I ask him as a special kindness to myself, he agree. But now that there is all this ugly trouble I have no right——"

"Wait!" I shouted at him. "Wait a moment! D'you mean to tell me—d'you mean to say you know——?"

"Sure," said a drawling voice from the doorway. We both turned.

Christopher Ingham, with Leofric on a chain beside him, lounged into the room.

"We made a mistake about that train," he said to Virag. "It doesn't run on Saturdays. There isn't one till three-ten."

"Very well, we go at three-ten," said Virag.

Ingham turned to me. He gave his lazy laugh.

187

"I suppose you got on to it through that parson," he said. "Well, it doesn't matter. I'm not a fugitive from justice, but only from men's nasty minds. I'd hoped to dodge them; I've grown tired of facing up to my past. If I haven't succeeded it's a nuisance, but there are no bones broken. I'm Charles Illstree all right."

I was staring at Virag. "And you knew it?"

"Naturally."

In small fragments, shattered to pieces, my theory crashed to the ground.

It left my mind a dull blank. Standing there between the two men I was not thinking lucidly. I was only aware that I had just been saved from making an awful fool of myself. Fumbling clumsily with my thoughts I recognised that if Virag knew all about Charles Illstree then Teed had no lever to force him to act as he wished; Teed, in fact, in the talk I had just had with him, had probably been sincere in all he had said. The only comfort was, I had not told my theory to anyone but George, and George is used to my making a fool of myself.

Ingham was saying: "As a matter of fact, it was Dr Virag's idea that I should pretend to be an American. I wasn't keen on coming here because I felt it was rather too near to some of my old haunts. But he said he couldn't manage without me, and as I owe more to him than to any other person alive, I didn't like letting him down. He suggested that with a different accent and nationality people wouldn't link me up with the vague memories they might still have. You see, I'd taken a risk soon after he employed me, and told him all the facts. I thought I'd sooner tell him myself than have someone do it for me. I could ask him straight out what he felt about it. . . . Well, I'm glad I took the risk. I stuck to my false name for general purposes, but apart from that I've been able to live the last three years without concealment."

"It was nothing to me," said Virag in an embarrassed tone. "You did your work well, I could not afford to lose you."

Ingham grinned at me. "He could have replaced me easily."

"It was all of no consequence," said Virag impatiently. "The court had acquitted you, and I have great respect for the English courts. Also I believed you. But I am sorry that by coming here for me you have again met with this old story."

I slumped down into a chair and held my head. I muttered: "But then in God's name, who? . . . And why? . . . *Why?*"

Virag went on: "We shall be travelling with the three-ten, Mr Dyke. Please inform me of my owing to you, and I will write a cheque."

"You don't owe me anything," I said, "I haven't found out anything. I haven't found out anything at all."

I got to my feet again and went towards the door. I went out into the hall and stood there wondering what evidence, what essential pieces in this puzzle I had overlooked.

I was turning to the stairs to go to my room and do some more hard thinking when there was a sudden rush of footsteps behind me. Marion Teed came in at the open door. She was moving with stumbling, panting haste. Her hair had come undone and hung in a coil over her shoulder; there was a dead beech leaf caught on the rough wool of her skirt; her breathing sounded as if it would burst her lungs. As she pushed past me and went running upstairs I saw that her face was as white as paper.

*　　*　　*　　*　　*

My room was full of sunshine. The french window stood wide open and the chalk walls enclosing the little garden had a dazzle in the brilliant light. As I came in and closed the door a bee buzzed in at the window and went humming about the room. I chased it out, then flung myself down on the bed. As the warm scent of flowers and honey drifted around me I closed my eyes. There was a drumming behind them and I knew that yesterday's headache was returning.

Perhaps because of that growing headache or perhaps because I had begun to feel very hungry, I found it difficult to concentrate. I tried going back to the beginning of the case; I thought over everything that had happened since George and I had arrived at Bule. But my mind played tricks with me; my thoughts went vague; accurate memories eluded me. The twinges behind my eyes were growing sharper. The trouble was, I had no means of knowing whether I had already collected all the significant pieces of the puzzle and had merely to find the right way of putting them together. or whether I had still to go grubbing in crannies and dark corners for missing pieces. Profound doubt of myself assailed me, and an unusual dislike of my occupation. If the Cricketers had been nearer I should have gone out for a drink; if I had remembered to buy cigarettes in the village I should have smoked; if George had been there I should have talked. But I had only my own company, my headache and the scent of the flowers to help me.

The torpor of discouragement into which I sank was almost as blank as sleep. The bee flew in again and buzzed over my forehead. At one point I had a feeling that footsteps had just gone past my door, and at one point I realised that I had heard a car drive off; I supposed it was Glynne going back to the village. My head and my stomach felt completely empty. Unfortunately, remembering Marion Teed's white face, I had no hope of a meal in the immediate future.

It was without any warning sound of footsteps in the passage that the door suddenly opened and George slipped inside. Sitting down quickly on the bed beside me, he thrust into my hands a woman's handbag of brown crocodile-skin.

" This was what," he said.

I took it uncertainly. " What was what? "

" This was what she was hidin'."

" Who was hiding where? "

" This was what Marion Teed was runnin' away to the wood to hide."

" When? "

" When I saw her and got out of the car. You mean you didn't see her? "

I sat up, rubbing my eyes. " I didn't see anybody."

" But that's why I got out of the car. Where's your eyes, Tobe? I knew Glynne didn't see her and a good job too, but I thought you'd seen her. She was runnin' off as fast as she could go towards the wood —and when she got there she got busy hidin' this."

" Why? "

" Pull yourself together, Tobe," said George sternly. " How could I know why? I ain't even taken a look inside it. I just waited till she'd finished buryin' it under some leaves and sticks, and then I waited until she got clear, and then I dug it up and brought it straight along."

" I'm damned hungry," I said, " and I wish I had an aspirin." I turned the bag over. It was old and shabby and slightly stained with moist earth, but it was of good quality, though a little too large and clumsily practical to be particularly handsome. It looked just the sort of bag a girl like Marion Teed would carry.

Yet I did not remember that I had seen her with it.

" Come on, come on, open it! " said George.

I snapped open the clasp.

Whoever the owner of the bag was, she was not the sort of woman who allows empty envelopes, shop-receipts, stubs of cinema-tickets, pencils with broken points, keys of the last house but one that she lived in and broken mirrors to accumulate in her bag. It was perfectly neat. There was a handkerchief, a cheque-book, a comb—but there were no cosmetics; there was a latch-key and a purse with seven pound notes in it and some silver; there were some safety-pins on a ring, and there was the return half of a railway ticket bought at Bule on the previous Monday. That was all there was in the bag except for one thing. That one thing was decidedly strange. It was a revolver.

It was a silly little revolver, a showy thing, a toy. But it had had one shot fired out of it.

George breathed hotly down my neck as he craned over my shoulder to see the contents of the bag. When he saw the revolver he gave an excited whistle.

The revolver was one of those improbable, pearl-mounted things, and it actually had a silver monogram on the butt. The initials of the monogram, ornately entwined, were two Ps and a B.

" Percy-bloody-Peach! " cried George.

" You're right," I said. I did not realise I had lost my headache and my hunger. " Percy Peach. . . . I'd forgotten all about him. Poor Percy. . . . But why a revolver, anyway, at this stage of the case? And whose bag is it? Not Mrs Peach's. She'd never carry a clumsy thing like that. And why did the Teed girl hide it in the wood? "

" Most likely because it's the only place hereabouts to hide anythin'," said George.

"The same reason as somebody took Leofric there."

" Oh," said George, " you agree about that now, do you? "

" I never said I didn't agree."

" But you kind of looked as if you was somewhat sceptical. You'd got your own ideas."

" I've no ideas now about anything."

I told him of my talk with Virag.

George chewed on the knuckle of his thumb and nodded at intervals. "That's right," he said once or twice, and as I finished: "That's right. I thought old man Virag probably knew all about Ingham. You see, Tobe, if you think it out——"

"Damn it, I did think it out!" I cried.

"That's right, Tobe. But you see—that trial of Illstree's was six years ago. Ingham said he's been workin' for Virag for three years. That means he'd had no time to acquire American citizenship. And *that* meant that he'd be travellin' still on a British passport. See what I mean?—'cos I don't believe a bloke could go travellin' around with another bloke, like Ingham's been doin' with Virag, and not let him catch a glimpse of his passport."

"He might have a faked one."

"'Tisn't so easy to get one if you don't know the ropes. Illstree was never one of the regular gang, he was just a bloke that got himself in a mess. No, Tobe. . . . Mind you, I wouldn't have said I was dead certain sure of it if you'd asked me, but I'd have said the odds were pretty good that Virag knew all about Mr Illstree's spot of bother."

"All right, all right," I said, "I'm a fool. Go on and say it."

"Oh no, you ain't a fool, Tobe. It's just that your mind works too fast, see? It don't leave you any time to think."

"And now Virag's clearing off," I said, "and I've failed, and in all fairness I can't take his money— which leaves my bank-balance in just the same condition as before, that's to say, in red ink, signifying overdrawn."

"Of course," said George thoughtfully, "the reason Virag's in such a hurry to be off and why he's made up his mind like he has not to take any of the old lady's money, is that he knows the girl's mixed up in it, and he doesn't want to have her shown up."

"What, Marti? But Marti was in the car with us when——"

"Oh yes, she was in the car with us all right when Irma was killed. But not when the chimps got out of their cages, was she?"

"But she couldn't have killed Irma."

"That's right, she couldn't have. But she could've been the one who let them escape in London, couldn't she? And she could've been the one who let them escape the next time. And she could've been the one who knew that if she didn't bring Ingham the cigarettes she'd promised, sooner or later he'd go and get them himself. And she was the one who was always borrowin' Mrs Peach's car, wasn't she? She could have waited and watched till she saw Ingham pop off to the village for his cigarettes, and then she could've run down to the garage, got the car out, pushed the animals into it—only Irma got away—and then she could've driven off. And she was the one who'd got a reason for it all."

"Yes," I said, "and I suppose she wouldn't even have thought she was harming her father. She'd have thought she was merely forcing him to take a good job. I suppose the idea was the chimps'd get loose and make trouble, and that the police'd then come down on Virag or Miss Miall and put a stop to the whole scheme. And she was probably thinking of the nice time she was going to have with the students when her father had to give in and go to America. Yes, she'd got a motive. And she's capable of doing a thing like that too. But she couldn't have killed Irma."

"I know she couldn't have," said George, "and her old man knows she couldn't have. What I reckon he thinks is that she paid someone to do it."

I grimaced. "Who'd be a parent? But is that what you meant, George, when you said you knew who'd done it and why?"

"No, Tobe, it ain't. The girl had nothin' to do with killin' the monkey."

"Well, what did you mean?"

George hesitated. He chewed his thumb again and looked broody and unhappy. After a moment he took his thumb out of his mouth and jerked it at the bag of crocodile-skin.

"Who d'you think that belongs to, Tobe?" he asked.

"You're doing the thinking now," I said. "Whose is it?"

He pointed at the return half of the railway ticket. "Don't that mean nothin' to you, Tobe?"

As I have said, the ticket had been bought at Bule on the previous Monday. This was the half from Waterloo to Bule. It had been punched but never collected. It looked as if the person, whoever it was, who had bought it, had gone on to the platform at Waterloo, then changed her mind, left the platform

196

again, and had somehow arrived at Bule by other means than train.

Waterloo. Monday.

Suddenly the facts clicked together in my mind.

"Rosa Miall!"

George nodded. "It's her bag all right, Tobe."

"Rosa Miall! . . . It was on Monday that she left for London to see Lord Nutlin. But how and when did she get back? And where the hell's she gone to now? And why's she got Percy Peach's revolver in her bag? And why did Marion Teed bury the bag? And why——?"

"Marion! Marion!"

The cry cut in on us from downstairs.

It was a shrill cry with an urgent ring of exasperation in it, as well as a curious note of alarm. Hurrying feet followed immediately upon the cry. Someone came running up the stairs and went past our door to one farther down the passage.

"Marion—where are you?" It was Katharine Peach calling out. "Marion—where are you? It's a quarter-past two and we're all nearly dead with hunger. Marion!"

George and I came out into the passage.

Katharine Peach, coming running out of Marion's room again, clutched at my arm. "Mr Dyke, where's Marion? Have you seen her?"

"She came upstairs and went to her room some time ago," I said.

"But she isn't there now."

Glynne came up the stairs. I realised then that it

could not have been he who had driven away in the car I had heard.

He walked past us and straight into Marion's room. After a moment he came out again. He was reading a note. His good-looking, nervous face went hard as he read, then he thrust the note into his pocket.

He looked round at us.

" She's gone, that's all," he said.

*   *   *   *   *

Virag and the others had heard the clamour and had come out of the sitting-room. We formed a group in the hall, all silent except Katharine Peach who was burbling in Glynne's ear : " But gone where, Kenneth? And why? What d'you mean, Kenneth —what d'you mean, gone? She can't just *go*. I mean, how are we to manage? She knows I'm no good at it. And besides—well, what *do* you mean, Kenneth? "

" Simply that she's gone," he said harshly. " How the hell should I know where—or how—or why? "

" But that note, Kenneth—— "

" I think," I said, " I heard her go. I heard steps in the passage and then a car driving away."

" How long ago? " asked Glynne.

" A car! " cried Katharine. " Whose car? "

" Yours, I imagine," I answered.

" But—— " She gaped at me pallidly. " Oh, she's got no right to do a thing like that! I never said she could have my car to run away in."

" How long ago did you hear her? " Glynne asked me again.

"Half an hour—three-quarters—I really don't know for certain."

He swore savagely.

"Perhaps it was your car she took, Kenneth," said Katharine Peach hopefully. "After all, you're engaged, and it isn't nearly such a wrong thing to do to pinch the car of someone you're engaged to as somebody else's."

"I'm not engaged to her," said Glynne. "She's just broken it off."

I saw the gleam in Katharine Peach's eyes. But she wailed at once: "Oh, Kenneth—oh, I *am* so sorry. And—oh, aren't we fools? Here we all are cluttering around you when, of course, the only thing in the world you want at the moment is to be left alone. Such terrible fools, all of us. Oh, I'm so, so sorry. But we didn't realise, did we, Mr Dyke——?" She turned to me, appealing to me with a flapping gesture of her bandaged hand.

But as she looked at me her sentence broke off in the middle and she gave a violent scream.

Glynne jumped as if he had been shot.

"Look!" gasped Katharine Peach.

She was pointing at the bag of crocodile-skin which I still held in my hand.

Silently I cursed myself for having brought it.

Virag said confusedly: "Please, what is the matter?"

"That bag," said Katharine, "it's Aunt Rosa's."

"So I thought," I said.

"But d'you mean——?" Her blue eyes swam

with apprehension; she breathed hard. "D'you mean she's here?"

"I haven't the least idea. I know it's her bag, that's all."

She stretched out her hand to take it.

I said: "If you don't mind, I'm rather looking forward to returning it to Miss Miall myself."

She turned to Glynne helplessly.

"Aunt Rosa's here," she said, "and Marion's gone, and that poor chimpanzee's been killed and we don't know who did it, and everything's upside-down, and Aunt Rosa'll say it's all my fault, because that's what she always says."

"Where did you find that bag?" Glynne asked me.

If I could have thought of a good lie I should have told it. I wanted to get their attention off the bag until I had had time to do some thinking about it myself. But what I told them was something near the truth.

"Oh, where everyone finds everything," I said airily, " in the wood."

Katharine Peach looked white and unsteady. I had not realised till then how afraid she was of her mother by adoption.

"I simply don't understand it," she said shakily. "When did you find it?"

"A little while ago."

Virag, in grave bewilderment, repeated once more: "Please, what is the matter?"

Glynne answered: "Miss Miall is somewhere in our midst—that's what's the matter." He laughed on a tired, dreary note. "I think I'd better go and see which of our cars Marion took. I'll be annoyed if it's mine; I've got all my things in it, and there's a round of calls I ought to be starting out on."

While Glynne was gone we moved from the hall into the drawing-room, and when he returned were standing about, uneasy and hungry, on the carpet that had been brought in from some other room to take the place of the bloodstained carpet that George had taken to the cleaner's. The new carpet was of a strong-minded shade of green that clashed stridently with the blue of the curtains.

Glynne told us it was the cream-coloured saloon that Marion had taken.

Marti Virag broke in excitedly: "But that still has some of our baggage in it."

"Is that so?" asked Virag quickly.

"I'm afraid so," said Ingham.

"That is very annoying—very," said Virag, clicking his tongue against his teeth. "There are notes of great value in one of my baggages."

"And we'll miss the three-ten," said Ingham.

I felt a tug on my sleeve. George was at my elbow, with a nod of his head he beckoned me out of the room.

"Say, Tobe," he whispered, "what's the betting that girl's at Bule station now, waitin' for the three-ten?"

I frowned. I began to say: "Why ever——?"

"Sh," said George, "don't let 'em hear. If there's a train at three-ten there won't be another for hours, will there?"

"But why should she go by train at all when

she's got a perfectly good car to get away in?"

"Because the car ain't hers."

I laughed.

"Sssh!" said George. He drew me out into the garden. "What I said ain't funny, Tobe. It's not as if she was you or me. Think of the kind of girl she is. She's never pinched anything in her life. She'd never run off in a car that wasn't hers, particularly if it'd got someone's valuable luggage in it."

"There's something in that," I said.

"Of course there is. That girl's at Bule station now, waiting for the train. And we want her back, Tobe."

"To tell us about the bag?"

"That's right. Now listen—if you pop down there quick, you can take the doctor's car and get to Bule before three-ten. Then you can tell her we've found the bag and that she's wanted at home to answer some questions about it."

"But she won't come."

"Don't tell me you can't get round that girl if you want to."

"And Glynne wants his car."

"That's why I'm tellin' you, be *quick*, Tobe! Take it quick before he can stop you." He gave me a shove.

"Well, why don't you go yourself, if it comes to that?"

"Because I shan't handle the girl as well as you will—you know that. And one of us has got to stay here and see that no one else goes away. I want to keep the whole lot of 'em here as long as I can manage it. Now will you get *movin'*? "

" George," I said, " what's on your mind? "

" For God's sake! " hissed George.

" Oh, all right," I said.

As I ran down the steps and got into Glynne's car I was hoping that amongst the patients I was preventing him from visiting that afternoon there were no cases of acute appendicitis or double pneumonia.

The road to Bule was white with dust, and the thick dust whitened the hedges. Heat-haze shimmered ahead of me. The only clouds in the sky looked as small and as tranquil as the sheep that grazed on the hillsides. Ideas were knocking at my brain again, but I was in no mood to be hospitable to them. Some of them had a decidedly fantastic air that I distrusted. At any rate I was too hungry to think.

But as the seven miles of road unwound over the rolling acres of dry turf, one of my ideas kept coming back to me and nagging at my mind with incredible persistence. I tried to dismiss the idea, yet found. myself examining it, checking it, elaborating it, and looking for answers to the questions that grew out of it.

The most important question was: why had Rosa Miall gone on to the platform at Waterloo, perhaps even taken her seat in the train, then changed her mind, and used some other means of transport for reaching East Leat?

By the time I reached the leafy valley of Bule I thought I knew the answer.

It was four minutes past three when I drove up to

the station. George had been right about the honesty of Marion Teed; she had not stolen the car. The cream-coloured saloon was parked in the station-yard next to the one rickety taxi. The girl herself was standing at the far end of the platform, waiting for the train. She was haggard and untidy. Her hat and coat looked as if she had thrown herself into them without a single glance in the mirror. She had no luggage.

She saw me coming. Hard and bright, her eyes blazed at me out of circles of deep shadow.

" Why have you followed me? " she demanded.

" To ask you to come back with me," I replied.

" You shouldn't have come. It was foolish." The tip of her tongue slid along her dry lips. " I've a right to go away if I want to."

" Yes, but all the same I wish you'd come back," I said.

" Why? "

I looked at the drawn skin of her face and into those blazing eyes. " Because if you go away in this sort of condition we're all going to feel rather uneasy about you."

" You needn't," she said stiffly.

" Nevertheless, we shall."

" What are you afraid of? That I'm going to commit suicide or something? "

" I think you're liable to do something mistaken, though I don't claim to know what."

She lifted her chin. " My condition's perfectly all right. I know what I'm doing."

" I'm afraid your appearance doesn't back that up."

"Well, it's none of your business."

"But why not come back with me to East Leat and take a little time to think it over?"

"Mr Dyke," she said sarcastically, "I'm not a lunatic. If I leave a place it's because I consider I have good reasons for leaving it."

"And if I come chasing a girl seven miles when I'm already faint with hunger, I've got good reasons too! You must be pretty hungry yourself, and you're overtired. You're really not in a fit state to grapple with the horrors of the local train-service. Why not come back and have a meal, and lie down, and get Dr Glynne to give you a bromide, and——"

"I've broken off my engagement with Dr Glynne."

"Well, what about it? That doesn't mean he can't give you a bromide."

"I don't want to see him again."

"Well, that's your affair. You needn't see him. But I think you ought to come back. After all, it's scarcely fair on Miss Miall, is it, dashing off like this without giving her any notice?"

She gave me a long, curious look. "Mr Dyke, what were your reasons for chasing me?"

Just then I heard the clatter of the signal dropping. I knew the train would be along in a moment.

"I've told you one of them," I said. "You aren't fit to travel. But also we want your help in solving the riddle of who stabbed Irma."

She laughed gratingly. "I don't think you're going to solve that riddle, Mr Dyke. You haven't gone the right way about it."

Distantly, I could hear the slow chug of the train.

205

" I shouldn't be too sure," I said.

Her dry lips curled. " You can't bluff me. You don't know anything. You don't know anything at all."

" And you do? "

She laughed again. " As if I should tell you! "

" Yesterday you said you were ready to help in any way you could."

" It was stupid of you to believe me."

I took hold of her by the arm. Far down the line I could see the smoke of the train. One or two other people had come out on to the platform.

I said : " I don't think it was stupid of me to believe you. Yesterday you meant what you said. But this morning you found out something——"

" Leave me alone, leave me alone! " She jerked her arm away from me. " Oh, why d'you keep on at me like that? Can't you see I want to be left alone? "

" Miss Teed, will you come back with me? "

" No! "

" Yesterday you were ready to help me find out who killed Irma, but today you made a discovery— today you yourself found out who did it. It's because you know and don't want to tell that you're running away——"

" Will you leave me alone? I don't care what you say, I'm going away. You can't stop me."

" Miss Teed, please—— "

" No, no, no! " Her voice rose shrilly above the clank and rumble of the train as it drew into the station. Almost before the train had stopped she had seized the handle of one of the doors and flung herself into a compartment.

I shrugged my shoulders. I had done my best.

As she settled herself by the farther window, she was panting slightly; the flesh of her face seemed to have fallen in against the bones. There was no one else in the compartment. I tried to convince myself that, as she had said, what she did was her own business. But seeing her sitting there, so white-faced and desperate, I could not get rid of the thought that in tomorrow's headlines I might read: " Girl Flings Herself from Train."

I remarked through the open doorway: " I suppose you're going to London? "

" Suppose what you like," she replied.

" It's a pity you're so loyal. Sometimes people aren't worth it."

She said nothing. Farther down the train the porter was slamming doors. I heard a whistle.

" I wish you'd change your mind," I said, " there's still time."

But even as I said it the train began to move.

" Goodbye, Mr Dyke," she said, with a small, tight-lipped smile. " Don't worry about me. I shall be all right. But I'm not coming back."

" At any rate," I said, walking beside the train, " you might tell me where you found that crocodile handbag you buried."

It was as if an electric shock had gone through the girl. My words seemed to throw her on to her feet. I saw the sudden opening of her mouth and the wildness in her eyes. The next moment she was out on the platform. The lurch of the train as she leapt flung her against me. She clutched at my arm.

"Did you say . . . a crocodile . . . ? "

The train was gathering speed.

"Good, then you're coming back," I said, " and on the way you can tell me where you picked up that handbag of Miss Miall's."

*　　*　　*　　*　　*

We drove back in Mrs Peach's car. I had wanted to return Glynne's car to him, but the girl refused to get into it. At first she refused to get into Mrs Peach's either; she still said she was not coming back. But her resistance had gone. In a few minutes we were on our way to East Leat. She sat beside me, holding her hat in her lap, rolling its felt brim with her thin, nervous fingers; the breeze through the open window tugged at her untidy hair.

I gave her a little time to recover herself, then I said: " Well, where did you find it? "

" Find what? " she asked stupidly.

" Miss Miall's handbag."

" I—I picked it up."

" Whereabouts? "

" I don't see why I should answer your questions," she retorted fretfully. " You aren't a policeman."

" I can get a policeman to ask you the same question if you'd prefer it."

" But you're here to find out about the chimpanzees, and this hasn't anything to do with them."

" I think it has."

" How can it have? "

208

"You know. That's why you were running away."

After a moment, as she said nothing, I asked again: "Whereabouts did you pick up the bag?"

"In the ditch," she replied with a sigh.

"By the side of the road?"

"Yes."

"Which ditch, what road?"

"Titmore Lane, of course. You see, I got tired of waiting for Kenneth—this morning, you know, in the village—so I decided to walk home, and I was walking along the road when a van passed and I had to get right over to one side. I was stepping across the ditch on to the grass when I saw something down in the ditch. I looked to see what it was and it was the handbag, and of course I knew at once it was Miss Miall's. . . ." She stopped, snatching an uncertain glance at me.

"And so you immediately went running off to the wood to hide the handbag?" I said.

She nodded.

"You must have done some quick thinking."

"I don't think I thought at all. I can see now it was very foolish of me."

"At any rate, you took a look inside the bag first, didn't you?"

"No," she said.

"But surely——"

"No," she said, tearing viciously at the felt brim of her hat, "no, no—I didn't!"

"The perfect secretary."

With a sigh, drearily, she said: "Oh well, it

doesn't matter to me if you don't believe me."

Again I waited a moment, then I said: "You know, Miss Teed, I believe you're suffering from an eclipse of your sense of proportion. Why should it be so important to conceal that Miss Miall's been here? Why not simply admit it? Why not admit you looked inside the bag and saw the revolver? After all, we all realise that Miss Miall's a somewhat singular individual. If once in her life she's performed a reprehensible action, we're all capable of remembering, I should think, her long life of worthy endeavour. And we're capable also of bearing in mind how worthy endeavour sometimes turns the brain a bit. Now tell me, you did look inside the bag and see the revolver, didn't you?"

"Oh well. . . . Yes, I did."

"And you know whom the revolver belongs to?"

"It's Percy Peach's. Didn't you see the initials on it? They stand for Percy Bretherton Peach."

"And where was that revolver generally kept?"

"Well, it was Katharine who brought it here, of course. She said it was to protect herself with in case Percy came here, but some time ago she gave it to Miss Miall, because she said it frightened her to handle it. Miss Miall put it in a drawer of her bureau."

"Which room is that in?"

"The drawing-room."

"Good," I said, "that fits."

"Mr Dyke. . . ." She hesitated. Pushing some hair out of her eyes, she looked round at me again.

Then suddenly she was groping for the handle of the door.

I grabbed her. "What the hell d'you think you're doing?"

"Please stop the car," she said. "I've changed my mind. I'm not coming back with you."

I accelerated. "You certainly are."

"I'm not. I was stupid to say I'd come. There's no reason why I should. I don't want to see—I don't want to see any of them again."

"You're coming back and you're going to tell Dr Virag where you found that bag."

"But I've already told you all about it." But she subsided in her seat. She seemed to be muttering to herself, for her lips kept moving, but she made no more sudden grabs at the door. When we reached the house she got quickly out of the car and without saying anything went straight upstairs to her room. I dodged Glynne and Mrs Peach and went looking for George.

I found him in the kitchen, sitting at the scrubbed, deal table, staring pensively before him. His gaze shifted round to me as I entered, but did not seem to take me in.

As I came across the room, however, he pushed a plate of sandwiches towards me.

"Here you are, Tobe, I saved these for you."

"Cheer up, George," I said, " we've got nothing to worry about. It's solved."

He watched me with deep melancholy as I fell on the food.

"That's right," he said, " it's solved."

"Oh," I said, "you've got there too, have you?"

"I got somewhere," he answered gloomily.

"Well, tell me about it."

"You tell me about yours first."

"It's so simple when you think of it," I said.

"That's right," said George.

"Of course, big ideas nearly always are simple."

"That's right."

"I mean to say, take Newton and the apple."

"I reckon that's been taken once too often," said George. "Go on, who did it?"

"Rosa Miall."

George jerked in his chair. His mouth dropped open.

"So that wasn't your idea?" I said. I grinned, for this time I was sure of myself.

"Lorlumme," said George, "it never even crossed my mind!"

"But it all hangs together," I said. "And when you think it out, it's not as fantastic as it sounds. One's apt to forget how unbalanced people of her sort frequently are. Living entirely on her conscience, as it seems she does, instead of mostly on her feelings, like the rest of us, she's undergoing a colossal strain all the time. Sooner or later a person like that is bound to crack."

"Go on," said George, "go on!"

"Well," I said, rapidly eating sandwiches, "it was by thinking about the return-half of Miss Miall's ticket to London that I got there. She came to East Leat—her bag proves that—but she didn't come by train. She——"

"Wait a minute," said George, "that bag. . . . Did you get the girl to tell you where she found it?"

"Yes, in the ditch, somewhere between here and the village."

"You mean it'd been there since some time yesterday?"

"Presumably. Well, as I was going to say, Miss Miall probably saw Lord Nutlin yesterday—probably had a final interview with him. She must have realised at last that it *was* a final interview. She'd reached her Moscow. Crushed, defeated, she retreated. She set off for Waterloo——"

"Say, Tobe, couldn't you leave the history out of it and just tell me what happened?"

"I'm telling you. She set off for Waterloo. She was in a sort of daze of rage and despair. She had her ticket punched at the barrier and she walked along the platform. She'd lost hope, she'd lost prestige, and, since she didn't intend to go back on her bargain with Virag, she'd lost a good deal of money. She could easily afford to lose it, but she'd spent a great deal of her life in poverty, and even when money was left to her, she'd never made much use of it—in other words, she'd never got accustomed to thinking in large sums. So when she started thinking of the amount she was to give away, and all for nothing, she was appalled. Probably that thought was only the last straw; by itself it wouldn't have made her do what she did; but when it came to her something suddenly snapped in her brain. In a flash she'd made up her mind to salvage something from the wreck. The chimpanzees were hers, but they were now of no use to her. Very well then, she'd kill them and at least get back the considerable sum for which they'd been insured."

"Gosh," said George, "it's fine. Go on."

I went on: "You know, when people are going through acute mental crises, their minds sometimes function with extraordinary rapidity and clarity. Miss Miall may still have been walking up the platform, or have been only a minute or two in her seat, when she realised that if she travelled by train everyone would know of her return. She'd arrive at Bule, she'd have to take a bus or a taxi, she'd be recognised; it wouldn't suit her purpose at all. So she left the station. I don't know what means she took of getting to East Leat, but probably she hired a car —yes, of course that's what she did. She hired a car and she drove straight down. I don't know whereabouts she stopped the car; she may have had the nerve to drive right up to the house itself. She wasn't expecting to find the chimps in the house, but she had to go in to fetch the revolver. In she went—very quietly—and found no one about. She got the revolver from the drawer of her writing-table in the drawing-room, and slipped the thing into her bag. And then, just as she was about to set off for the garage, in came Irma. I don't know where Irma had been hiding while the hunt was up; she must have found a coal-hole or something where no one had thought of looking—anyway, there she was, and there was Miss Miall facing her with murder in her heart and a gun in her handbag."

As I paused, George chortled with enthusiasm and rubbed his hands. I took the last sandwich.

"You've got to remember," I said, "that Miss Miall's somewhat unhinged mind was still working at top speed. She realised a gun was likely to be heard. But there was a sharp-bladed dagger in the china-cabinet, and Irma had thoughtfully brought along a piece of bamboo. Miss Miall coaxed the bamboo away from Irma and found that the hilt of the knife fitted beautifully into the end of the bamboo. I can see her chuckling gleefully over her horrible weapon—then she stabbed the poor beast. Then she went back to the car. She must have driven on into the village, and probably the door of the car wasn't properly latched and swung open; when she jerked it shut she didn't notice that her bag had fallen into the ditch. I suppose she took some other road back to London, or wherever it is she's gone. And I'm ready to bet that by now she's either gone right over the edge and is completely off her head, or else she's being eaten up with conscience and misery. And in either case I think Virag's perfectly right that it'll be best for everyone if none of us does anything more about the matter. However, having solved his case for him, thank heaven we haven't got to say no-thank-you when he tries to give us his cheque!"

For some reason, as I finished, the enthusiasm faded from George's eyes. I have long ago given up trying to guess from his expression what he is thinking; his face tells you about as much as one of those faces made out of rubber sponge.

He sat scratching the inside of one ear.

"Reckon you must have had a bit of a mental crisis yourself to think of all that," he said after a moment.

"Oh, I don't know," I said. "Once an idea gets me it won't let me go."

"That's just the trouble. . . ." He was frowning. "But what about why she moved the monkey?"

I pounded the table. "That's just the bit that clinches it!"

"You don't say."

"Listen, George, didn't you say yourself we'd gone wrong about that?"

He nodded.

"Well, we did go wrong," I said. "I admit it. I admit I went ahead too fast. I jumped to the conclusion that there could only be one reason why Irma was moved, and that reason was that the killer was trying to remove the body by the window but had to give it up because he was interrupted by our arrival. If that had been correct it would have meant that Irma had been dead only two or three minutes when we found her and that the killer was somewhere close at hand. But that wasn't what happened. Miss Miall had come and gone before we ever got here."

"Yes, but why did she move the monkey?"

I laughed. I thumped him on the chest. "George, don't you ever look around you?"

He looked irritated. "You know I do."

"Well, when you look around you in this house," I said, "what do you see?"

" Same as in most places."

" No, George, that's where you're wrong. In most places all you see are walls, windows, furniture. But here what stares at you from every polished surface is fanaticism. Can't you see it? There's pure passion gone into the way this house has been cleaned. There's a whole attitude to life expressed in the way the floors shine and the brass gleams. It's cleanliness next to godliness all right—in fact, it's cleanliness all mixed up in godliness. Now don't you see what I'm getting at? When Miss Miall stabbed Irma she was sufficiently wrought up to overlook the fact that Irma's blood would gush out on to the carpet. She did the deed, and out came thick, red blood where before there'd never been even an overturned ashtray. You can imagine how sheer horror would grip the old lady. You can see her leaping forward to drag Irma off the carpet."

" But then why *didn't* she drag her off the carpet? "

" Because you can have a carpet cleaned, but it's impossible to scrub blood off a polished floor without ruining the polish. As soon as she'd started to drag Irma away, Miss Miall realised that it was really much better to leave things as they were. Now is there anything else you want to know? "

" Yes," said George, " what happened to the bullet? "

" What bullet? "

" The one that was fired out of the gun? "

" Since it wasn't fired into Irma it's no concern

217

of mine," I said. I got up. "I'm going along now to talk to Virag."

"To tell him all this?"

"Why not?"

"It's just that . . . You know, Tobe, it rained in the night, but that handbag of Miss Miall's wasn't wet at all, so Miss Teed wasn't tellin' you the truth about where she found it."

"Oh hell"—I was on my way to the door—"you just want to be obstructive. But you can come along with me to Virag and get your share of the credit—and the cheque. You've done your share of the job all right; it was very useful the way you cleared up the fact that there wasn't any connection between the killing and the way the animals kept escaping."

"Yes, but, Tobe——" He was trotting behind me. "I say, Tobe——"

But I was looking for Virag.

He was not in the sitting-room. Through its window, however, I caught sight of him wandering up and down in the garden. With his hands linked behind him and his head bent, he looked serenely deep in thought. Since making up his mind as to his own course of action, I believe he had ceased to be disturbed by or even interested in the problem of Irma's death.

As we approached round the house he stood still and composed his features with an air of great patience, but his lack of interest was obvious.

I began: "Dr Virag, we've come to tell you that we've found the solution——"

But at that point George, grabbing me by the arm

and digging the tips of his fingers into it, said: "Dr. Virag, me and Tobe just come to tell you that we're goin' for a walk. We won't be long."

Virag bowed slightly, though he looked surprised.

Before I could speak again George blundered on: "You've missed your train, Dr Virag, so I suppose you can't be in any hurry, and so, if you wouldn't mind, there's somethin' I'd like to ask you to do while we're gone. We'd like you to keep an eye on Miss Teed."

"Miss Teed?"

"She's up in her room now," said George. "It might be—important."

Virag considered him for a moment. "What do you wish me to do?"

"See that she don't speak to anyone, and that no one don't try to speak to her."

"Very well, I sit on the stairs, then no one goes upwards or downwards," said Virag.

"And maybe you might ask Mr Ingham to stay outside her window?" said George.

"If you wish."

"Thanks," said George. "Now come along, Tobe, you and me had better get goin'."

I waited until we were round the corner of the house and then I told him what I thought of him. I started off well; I was angry, I was bewildered, and the condition gave me fluency. But as George merely gave me a broody look and set off down the steps to the gate, I, following, fell silent. I have often told George what I think of him and it has never done any good; I suppose I have become discouraged.

"Anyway," I said peevishly after a few minutes, "why have we got to go walking? I don't want to go walking. I can always think best sitting down."

"We got to walk," said George, trotting over the turf, "because we're goin' to look for somethin'."

"What? Where? I wish you'd tell me what's on your mind, George."

"I would, Tobe—I would if I was sure. But maybe I gone just as wrong as you. I been arguin' from certain pre-mises, and they do *seem* to check up like, and yet maybe they don't. So I want to prove it to meself before I start tellin' anyone else about it. If I'm right, I know who killed Irma and why, and why the stain of blood was the shape it was, and where Marion Teed really found the handbag. . . . But first I'm goin' to prove it. And to prove it I got to find somethin', and I reckon the place I'll find it in is in the wood."

"Why the wood?"

"For the same reason as Marti Virag took Leofric there yesterday, and Marion Teed took Miss Miall's handbag there. It's the only place hereabouts where you can hide a thing."

"But what is it you're looking for?"

He gave me an uncertain glance, his pink face puckered with thought. I thought he was not going to answer, but at length he grunted reluctantly: "Well, if you got to know—I'm lookin' for that bullet."

*   *   *   *   *

Fortunately it was a nice wood.

It was quite a pleasure to sit down on a fallen log and to look at the blue shimmer of the sky through the beech leaves.

I had no intention of searching for bullets in beechwoods until I had had some practice with needles in haystacks.

As George went stamping over ferns and brambles, treading them down and catching his clothes on the thorns, I lit a cigarette and leant back against the great trunk of the tree behind me. Warm shafts of sunlight gilded the undergrowth. A few inches in front of my face a caterpillar was sinking to the earth on a long, silken strand that caught the sunshine and gleamed like a thread of gold.

The trees were all squat, thick-bodied giants, centuries old. They stood far apart from one another, only the tips of their boughs intermingling; I could see almost from end to end of the wood between their silvery trunks. On the ground there was a thick, copper carpet of beech leaves. A few weeks earlier the place would have been a mass of blue-bells.

The caterpillar swayed in mid air. Its soft, green body wriggled and turned, and I wondered if it could ever spin enough thread out of itself to reach the ground. George's footsteps sounded farther and farther away. Over my head I could see a haze of midges, making a speckled, wavering mist against the light.

Perhaps I sat there for twenty minutes; it may have been longer. I had smoked a cigarette and had

trodden the stub of it into the earth; I had stopped
thinking about anything; the caterpillar had vanished, and I had had a glimpse of a squirrel, and for
several minutes had watched a butterfly of chalky
blue flickering around me. . . .

Suddenly I heard George's shout.

It came from far over on my left and there was
a high note of urgency in it. I was on my feet in a
moment, running.

But there was no need to hurry. George himself
was not hurrying. When I found him he was standing still with his back to me, looking down at the
ground. He heard me coming and looked round.
His pink face had a curiously grey look and there
were small, deep wrinkles round his eyes. As I
joined him he pointed down at the earth.

The wood was a nice wood no longer.

George had found the bullet.

VII

ONE OF US had to stay there while the other went
for the police. George said he would sooner stay.
But before I set off for the village George and I
talked. Time was precious, so we talked fast, only
skimming the details, but we made a plan. It was a
faulty plan, for though it was obvious now who had
killed the chimpanzee and why, certain things were
not going to be easy to prove.

"But look here, George," I said just before starting off, "why don't you go yourself and fetch the
police and then go on and do the rest of it? It's
you who've solved the whole thing."

"No, Tobe, I don't fancy havin' to do a lot of
talkin'. You go," said George.

So I went. I did not go to the police-station, but
put through a hasty call to Sawbry from the call-box
round the corner. While I was talking I heard other
voices dimly behind the sergeant's and guessed that
the inspector from Ashingham, of whom Sawbry
had spoken, must have arrived. I said enough to
send several policemen racing for the beechwood.
Then I myself set off up Titmore Lane. I walked
rapidly, and suddenly, as I left the village, found
that I was in a very bad temper. I had just remembered something, something that George and I, as
we talked in the wood, had forgotten to discuss,

something that would have been a great deal of help to me at the moment.

I had just remembered the carpet.

Kicking at a stone in the road, I swore viciously. I had known that carpet would turn out to be important, but I had not guessed how important. George had made an enormous mistake in taking it to the cleaner's.

"You look very thoughtful, Mr Dyke. Is anything the matter?"

I looked up to find the vicar addressing me from his usual resting-place by the roadside. He was smoking his usual cigarette.

"I've been watching you approaching," he went on wheezily. "Your face struck me, if you don't mind my saying so, as looking uncommonly serious."

"Something very serious has happened," I replied.

"Ah," he said, "I feared so."

"Why?" I asked, frowning. I was wondering whether the police would be able to get hold of the carpet before it underwent the cleaning process.

"Well, as I was resting here," said the vicar, getting laboriously to his feet, "I saw our worthy Sawbry and some other gentlemen in blue uniforms running as fast as they could towards the wood. I've never seen Sawbry run so fast except on an occasion when his own bicycle was stolen. Is it an accident, Mr Dyke?"

"Unfortunately, no," I answered.

"You don't mean——?" He shot a shrewd

glance at me. "You don't mean something's happened to the other chimpanzee?"

"Not that I know of," I said.

"Ah well," he said after a moment, "if you don't want to tell me, don't. I daresay I shall learn all about it as soon as is good for me. You're going on to the house?"

"Yes," I said, "and I'm rather in a hurry. So if you don't mind . . ."

"Ah," he said, "so am I, so am I. So perhaps you'd be so very kind as to loan me an arm. I always find the last part of this hill very trying." He took possession of my arm. "May I ask if you've been to Ashingham yet, and managed to get a call through to Lord Nutlin?"

"No," I said. As we went up the hill I had to slow my pace down to suit his. "No, I haven't been into Ashingham, and as a matter of fact—— Well, I'd better apologise straight away for my suspicions, Mr Teed. They were quite unfounded."

"Ah, I'm so glad to hear you say that," he said.

"And I'm extremely sorry——"

"Not at all, not at all. Not another word about it. No doubt I struck you as a very suspicious character." The huge man gave his coy, little titter in my ear. "May I ask if you exonerated me because you discovered a fallacy in your argument, or because you've found definite proof that someone else is to blame?"

"I hope it's definite proof," I replied.

"Dear, dear," he said, and his big, yellow face went suddenly thoughtful. He said no more, only his hand on my arm seemed at each step to weigh me down more heavily. Our pace was a snail's crawl. But though I fumed with impatience, I found myself feeling half-grateful for the delay.

Before we entered the house I caught the sound of Glynne's voice, raised, arguing angrily with someone in the hall. The other person turned out to be Virag. He was sitting halfway up the stairs and, with a book open on his knees and an expression of courteous firmness on his face, was refusing to get out of the way.

" No, Dr Glynne," he was saying quietly, " I regret, but I engage to sit here so no one go upwards or downwards. I do not know why I am required to do it, but I promise I stay, so I stay. Have you read this book? It is a very interesting book on the decline of scientific activity in the second century before Christ. It is tinged with Marxism, but still very interesting. The writer contends that———"

" Dr Virag," said Glynne tensely, " are you going to let me go upstairs? "

" No, Dr Glynne. As I was saying, the writer contends that it was not in the interests of the aristocratic class to permit the natural sciences to———"

" Dr Virag, are you going to let me go upstairs to talk to my fiancée? " shouted Glynne dangerously.

I said, behind him: " I thought she wasn't your fiancée any more? "

As Kenneth Glynne swung round I noticed how ravaged his face looked. He shouted at me: " What the hell's happening? Why can't I go upstairs and talk to Marion? Who told that old fool to sit there?

If he doesn't get out of the way I'll damn well throw him out of the way."

I said: "I shouldn't."

"I'll do it if he doesn't get out of my way!"

"If Marion's upstairs," observed the vicar, "she can undoubtedly hear your voice, my dear Kenneth. Therefore, if she doesn't put in an appearance, it must be because she isn't anxious to see you."

Glynne swore at him, then turned on Virag again: "Are you going to let me pass?"

I jerked Glynne back.

"Don't be a fool," I said. "We've got our reasons for handling things like this. And she isn't your fiancée any more. You said yourself she'd broken it off."

His arm in my grip was trembling. His eyes looked hollow and dark. "Don't you want to give me a chance to put things straight with her?"

"I thought you'd some patients to visit this afternoon," I said.

"So I have, but somebody's pinched my car." His voice went peevish: "I don't understand it—Marion went off in Katharine's car and then she came back. No one told me she'd come back; if I hadn't gone out in the garden and caught a glimpse of her at her window, I shouldn't even know she was back. And then that tough Ingham wouldn't let me get near the window. But anyway, she did come back, and brought Katharine's car back—and now it's my car that's gone. Where's it gone? Who's taken it? I don't understand it. What's been happening?"

I drew him towards the door. I said: "I'm afraid

I took your car to fetch Marion back in, but for some reason she wouldn't come back in it, so I brought her back in Mrs Peach's. Your car's parked at Bule station. But about those patients of yours——"

"Damn you, all my stuff is in my car!"

"Still, you could take Mrs Peach's, couldn't you?"

"But I tell you, all my things——"

"Glynne," I said sharply—I had got him out on to the steps—"I should take Mrs Peach's car if I were you."

"But why——?"

"Because it's faster than yours."

We eyed one another for a moment. The sunshine was warm and bright on the hillside and there was a lark's song in the air.

"And it's a nice afternoon for driving," I added. "I've just been walking myself—in the beechwood over there."

There came a change in Glynne's face. There was a slight relaxing of his features, a smoothing out of the lines of nervous tension. But the colour of his skin was ashen.

"I suppose it might be a good idea," he murmured.

"You can bet it's a good idea."

We were going down slowly, step by step, towards the gate.

"All right," he said, after another moment of brooding, "I'll take Katharine's car, and you can tell her——"

"I shouldn't worry about that."

He gave me another long look in the eyes.

"All right," he said, "don't tell her anything Funny—I thought you were a fool. Watching the way you were going to work I never thought you'd get anywhere." He got into the car. Suddenly he grinned crookedly. "I'm a conscientious physician, aren't I, Dyke, going to see my patients at a time like this? I was very conscientious last night about Jessie Warrell and her baby, wasn't I? I wonder if the brat'll turn out to have been worth it. Probably not—there's bad blood in this village all right. Remember that, Dyke. Mental deficiency and drunkenness. Miss Miall was right about those things in a way, only she was too crazy herself to find the right way of coping with them. But remember, you can't be any better than the stuff you're made of. . . . God, I'm tired, bloody tired."

"If you stay you'll probably find the proceedings here quite a strain," I said.

"No doubt." He reached for the brake. As the big car started silently down the hill he still had that crooked grin on his face. That grin is one of the memories of the case of the slaughtered chimpanzee that has stayed in my mind with the most haunting distinctness, and is the memory of which I should most like to be free.

I found Virag still sitting on the stairs.

I said: "If you don't mind, I'd like everyone to come into the sitting-room. I've something very important to say to you all."

Silently, except for Leofric, who arrived hand in hand with Ingham and who seemed to have a good

229

deal to say in his own way on the situation, they collected in the sitting-room. Marion and Katharine sat at opposite ends of the room, ignoring one another. They ignored one another in very different ways; Marion kept her gaze hard and straight before her and her shoulder ostentatiously turned towards the other woman; Katharine faced the room but kept her gaze dreamily on a corner of the ceiling. Marti sat next to her father. Virag had stopped reading about the decline of science in the second century before Christ, but still had a finger thrust between the pages of his book, marking the place. The vicar sat next to Marion, and because he was not allowed to smoke in Rosa Miall's house began pulling to pieces the upholstery on the arms of his chair.

I stood in front of the empty fireplace. I had put the crocodile-skin handbag down at one end of the mantelpiece.

I began: "You all know that I've been trying to discover who was guilty of the crime of stabbing Irma the chimpanzee. I now know who was guilty. Also I know how the crime was done and why. I should like, if you don't mind, to describe to you some of the steps by which I arrived at my solution of the problem. I should like to explain some of the mistakes I made, and I should like to ask one or two of you a few more questions."

I glanced round. Virag nodded his head in agreement, but amongst the rest there was a curious stillness.

"All right," I said, "I'll proceed." I propped myself against the mantelpiece. "In my first approach to the question of who stabbed Irma I concentrated on two aspects of the crime. I concentrated on a possible motive, and I concentrated on the strange shape of the stain made by the blood that had flowed from the wound. You'll all have noticed that the stain was much too long; if Irma had simply been stabbed and left where she fell, the stain would have been much smaller and rounder. But that long stain, which looked as if the blood must actually have trickled several feet along a horizontal and highly absorbent surface, suggested that Irma had been moved immediately after she was killed and then been dropped again. That, anyway, was my first explanation of the phenomenon. I believed that the killer had been trying to get her out through the window and had been interrupted. As a matter of fact, that explanation was a complete mistake. Irma was not moved after she was killed."

I thought Virag was going to say something, but he checked himself. I noticed that except for Katharine Peach, who went on staring at a corner of the ceiling, they were all looking at the carpet at the point where the stain had been.

I went on: "I was equally mistaken in my first approach to the question of motive. I'm afraid I got the whole thing wrong. The fact is, I succumbed to the temptation of thinking much too anthropomorphically. I found motives of jealousy and greed and anger—motives that would have suited the case if Irma had been a human being. For instance, Irma was insured: thus Dr Virag might have killed her, as Smith killed his brides in the bath. Then

Irma stood between Mrs Peach and a considerable sum of money; I considered the possibility that Mrs Peach might have killed her for that reason. Then Marti Virag was jealous of Irma, believing that the chimpanzees had more of her father's affection than she had herself; she might have killed Irma to be rid of a rival. Then Marion Teed was afraid that her fiancé might leave his work here and join Dr Virag in Tobago; you can call that a jealousy-motive too. Then the Reverend Alexander Teed feared the apes; he feared them for what it was in their power to bring about. Thinking in these terms, you see, each of these people had a motive. Christopher Ingham too, though he appeared to have no direct motive, might have been blackmailed by someone with knowledge of his past to do the killing."

As I paused I caught a faint grin on Ingham's face.

"Yes," I said, "I know that to each of you the thought that you might be thought capable of cold-bloodedly killing a sweet-natured chimpanzee for any of the motives I've mentioned probably seems ridiculous in the extreme. And I pretty soon found out myself that the motives wouldn't work out. No one, in fact, had a hold over Christopher Ingham, because Dr Virag already knew all about Ingham's past; Mrs Peach knew that Miss Miall's deal with Dr Virag had already gone through, so that the money was lost to her anyway; Dr Virag himself knew this, and wasn't likely to endanger the deal for the sake of the much smaller amount he'd get for the insurance; besides, like his daughter, he was in the car with George and me when Irma was killed; lastly,

Mr Teed knew that Lord Nutlin was not going to yield to Miss Miall's persuasions——"

"Lastly?" broke in Marion Teed suddenly, her voice sounding oddly loud, and its loudness seeming to startle her, for she repeated immediately, almost inaudibly: "Lastly—why d'you say lastly?"

"Yes, I know I've left out two people," I replied. "That's because, thinking in the way I was at the time, the five people I've named were the only ones who seemed to me to have motives. Later, it's true, I considered the fact that Miss Miall herself had a motive of a sort—but that didn't work out either. You see, as I've just found out, the motive for Irma's killing had nothing in common with any motive for killing a human being. Irma, in fact, was killed because she was a chimpanzee—or, to be more precise, Irma was killed *simply because she wasn't a human being*."

Virag shook his head gloomily. "I don't understand," he said, "I don't understand."

"But it's really very simple," I said. "The law doesn't take the death of a chimpanzee very seriously. Perhaps it'd fine the killer; it might even imprison him; but it certainly wouldn't hang him by the neck until he was dead. And so if there happens to have been a murder, and if there happen to be indelible traces of that murder, such as blood on a carpet, to give the show away, how could you conceal them better, and how could you better distract attention from what had actually happened, than by providing more blood and another body— in this case the blood and body of a chimpanzee?

Blood is the best disguise for blood. It was Dr Glynne who killed Irma. He did it in a desperate attempt to disguise the fact that Rosa Miall had been murdered in this room."

*   *   *   *   *

Katharine Peach stirred. Her gaze flickered down from its ceiling refuge and plunged straight into mine. A queer little moaning sound came through her lips. Then she sat upright in her chair.

"I don't believe it. Aunt Rosa—dead?"

Marion Teed bent her head and pressed her hands more tightly together.

The others took their time to digest the information I had just given them.

"You tell us, you are serious, Miss Miall is dead?" said Virag.

"Yes," I said, "Rosa Miall was murdered yesterday in this room some time between about seven-forty-five and eight-fifteen. Her body has just been discovered in the beechwood. It was put there during the night—put there, I imagine, simply to get it out of the way until there was time to give it more effective burial. It was under scarcely six inches of earth, with leaves strewn on top in an attempt to hide the signs of digging. I think the body would have been removed from there tonight if it had not happened to be found by George. As it is, the police are busy removing it now."

"But——" the vicar began hoarsely. Then suddenly he tore open a packet of cigarettes and shot one of them into his mouth. I lit a match for him.

" But if she was killed here," he breathed through a mouthful of smoke, " how did she—how is it her —her body has just been found in the wood? "

I looked round the group.

" Would anyone else like to explain? "

There was a silence.

" What about you, Miss Teed? "

The girl shuddered.

" Well, you, Mrs Peach? "

" Oh, poor Aunt Rosa, poor Aunt Rosa! " was all I got out of the blonde woman.

" Either of you could explain this if you would," I said.

At that Mrs Peach exclaimed: " Why, you know I'm never any good at explaining anything, even something I understand . . . And this—this terrible thing . . ."

" Please, Mr Dyke, explain the matter to us," said Virag impatiently. " I do not understand." He looked as if a failure to understand caused him a sensation of acute discomfort.

" All right," I said, " but it isn't easy to know where to begin. Perhaps it'd be best if I started with a few questions. Mr Teed, would you mind telling again how many people you saw pass as you were sitting by the roadside yesterday evening? "

" Very well," he said. " I saw Mrs Peach come up the hill with a parcel under her arm. I saw Dr Glynne go down the hill in his car. I saw Mr Ingham, with one chimpanzee, returning from the wood. That's all I saw."

" You're absolutely sure that's all? "

"Absolutely sure."

"Thanks," I said, "then here's another question. D'you remember when you first heard that one of the chimpanzees was dead you leapt to the conclusion that it had been shot? I'd like you to think that over very carefully. Had anything happened to make you leap to that conclusion?"

"I see what you mean," he said. "Had I heard a shot?" He sucked in some of the soothing smoke. "Well, I had and I hadn't. That's to say, I'm not certain if I had or not. But certainly, as I was coming up the hill and was just about to sit down at my usual resting-place, I did hear a sound, and I thought to myself vaguely that someone was out shooting, then I thought more probably it was a car backfiring, and then I forgot about it. But when you mentioned that one of the chimpanzees was dead I suppose I automatically associated the sound I had heard with your information."

"I see," I said. "Well, I think you did hear a shot, and I think it was the shot that killed Rosa Miall. It was fired out of a revolver which used once to be the property of Mr Percy Bretherton Peach, but which had been kept for some time in a drawer of that bureau there." I pointed. "That's right, isn't it, Mrs Peach? Your husband's revolver was generally kept there?"

"Yes," she murmured, "but oh—oh, isn't it horrible?"

"It is," I agreed, "horrible. Well, when Miss Miall was shot—at very close range so that half her face was blown away—she fell to the ground, her

236

blood gushing out on to the carpet. Dr Glynne is a man of considerable intelligence. He knew there was no time to be wasted in removing the body——"

"But wait, Mr Dyke!" cried Marti Virag. Her plump little face was chalky pale. "How can it be as you say when Dr Glynne only arrived at the house at the same time as we did? Don't you remember, as we came round the corner he was just getting out of his car?"

"I'm afraid he wasn't," I said. "As we came round the corner he was *sitting* in his car. As soon as he saw us he got out and proceeded to act as if he were just arriving. But if, in fact, he had only just arrived, Mr Teed would have seen him drive *up* the hill as well as down it, wouldn't he?"

Marti turned swiftly to the vicar. "You saw him, Mr Teed!"

Teed shook his head. "I fear not, Miss Virag."

I went on: "Well, as I was saying, Glynne's a man of uncommon ability in certain directions. I'm sorry about him; it's a great waste. When he saw Miss Miall lying there dead he didn't lose any time. I imagine he wrapped her battered head in something to prevent the dripping of blood on the steps, then he carried her straight down to his car, pushed her into the back of it, covered her with a rug, and then went back to see what he could do about the stain of blood on the carpet. I don't know what he was thinking of doing about it. He couldn't have scrubbed it out in time. The only thing I'd have thought of in his place, I believe, would have been setting fire to the carpet. I rather think that

that was what he was intending to do, because when we arrived one of the oil lamps in here was already alight, although it was still broad daylight. I think he'd lit it, meaning to smash it just over the stain—but at that point, like an answer to a prayer, in came Irma. I don't know where she'd come from; she must have been somewhere in the house while the search was on, and I daresay the noise of the shot frightened her out of her hiding-place. Perhaps Glynne caught sight of her in the garden, or perhaps she actually came in here. At any rate, he'd done some work on chimpanzees before and was used to handling them. He coaxed her to the spot where he wanted her, then he took her piece of bamboo away from her and fitted the hilt of the little Chinese dagger in the cabinet into one end of the bamboo. Then he stabbed her. . . . You know, Glynne's a brave man as well as a clever one. Every instant he remained in this room he was taking a deadly risk. I'm sorry for him. He was a man in the toils. Well, as I was saying, he stabbed Irma and Irma's blood flowed out on to the carpet. But unfortunately for him he'd placed her badly, and when she fell her blood didn't flow directly over Miss Miall's, as he'd intended; instead it flowed beside it. The two stains joined into one stain, but a stain that was much too long. It was the shape of the stain that upset the whole plan—that and the fact that last night Jessie Warrell had a baby."

Marti Virag again interrupted: " Then you mean, Mr Dyke, that when we got out of the car and stood in the road talking to Dr Glynne, Miss Miall—the body of Miss Miall—was there in his car all the time?"

I nodded.

She drew a shuddering breath.

"And he didn't like it at all, if you remember," I said, "when you went and stood near to him. He was all on edge, and he hurried us to the gate. Then, in here, he made the suggestion as early as he could that he should go for the police, and he went to fetch them with the body of Miss Miall still in his car. But he didn't return here in his car; I remember when I saw him go back to the village late yesterday evening he went on foot, taking the path over the hill. I imagine that after calling at the police-station he'd driven his car into his garage and locked it in, and I imagine he was intending to go a long drive last night and get rid of the body a long, long way from here. But when he got back to his house he found a message that he was wanted at the Warrells'. . . . He was kept at the Warrells' all night. He'd only time before morning to put the body somewhere close at hand. He chose the wood presumably because in this open countryside it was the only place where he could be sure he wasn't being watched at his digging. But it was a bad choice, because it was the obvious place for us to look as soon as we realised what we ought to be looking for. And when he knew that I'd come back from the wood a short time ago, he knew the thing was finished."

"It's a pity," said Virag, "it's a pity. Intelligence is rarer than it should be. Dr Glynne must possess a remarkable degree of practical intelligence. Where is he now? "

I hesitated. Then I said : " Visiting some patients, I believe."

Virag looked as if he understood. " But I have noticed, Mr Dyke," he went on, " you tell us only of Dr Glynne's actions after the shot was fired that killed Miss Miall. Am I right that the meaning of that is that it was not Dr Glynne who fired the shot? "

" Quite right," I answered.

Teed exclaimed.

" But how did you know this? " asked Virag.

" Precisely because Glynne was intelligent."

" But I do not understand——"

" Listen," I said, " the murder of Miss Miall was a very foolish action. It was unpremeditated and impulsive; there was no thought in it of the inevitable consequences. Someone snatched the revolver out of the drawer of the writing-desk, and in hate, resentment, revenge and fear, fired. . . . All Kenneth Glynne's actions were a desperate attempt to save that person from the consequences of her senseless fury, her lack of foresight, her sheer stupidity. Oh, it was a very unthinking, foolish individual who did the murder, it wasn't Kenneth Glynne. He merely happened to be passionately in love with her. Mrs Peach "—I turned to her—" why were you so very stupid as to shoot Miss Miall? "

*　　*　　*　　*　　*

From where I was standing I could see all the

small movements they made. I could see the slow relaxing of Marion Teed's muscles, the quick turn of Virag's head, the lifting of Ingham's eyebrows. I could see the pulse beating in Katharine Peach's slender throat.

"I?" she said—a long, vague, incredulous monosyllable.

I nodded.

"B-but—why, I thought you were going to say it was Marion! You must mean it was Marion, Mr Dyke. It's her Kenneth's in love with—and besides, everyone knows she's a bit mad, all inhibitions and everything. I've always thought her a most desperately unstable sort of person, though of course I didn't say that to other people because I didn't want them to start thinking things about her, but all the same . . ."

She was saying too much and saying it too quickly. She must have realised it, for she stopped abruptly. Her lovely mouth stayed gaping a little.

"No," I said, "it isn't Miss Teed Glynne's in love with—as she knows."

"Oh, how can you say such a thing?" gasped Katharine.

As Marion Teed smiled wearily, I turned to her.

"Miss Teed, d'you mind if I go on? This may be painful for you."

She gestured indifferent assent.

I turned back to the other woman. "Dr Glynne is passionately in love with you, and you, in your way, with him. And the whole village has been talking about it for some time. That," I said,

" wasn't going to do either of you any good, because sooner or later Miss Miall was bound to hear about it too. The vicar's told us Miss Miall hadn't any tolerance towards the sins of the flesh, and until your divorce was concluded she would undoubtedly have insisted on regarding you as a married woman. If she knew that you were acting, as she considered, improperly, she was more than likely to turn you out. She'd done it once already when you made a marriage she disapproved of, and she was quite capable of doing it again. You knew that if your affair with Glynne was discovered you stood to lose comfort and wealth and all hope of inheriting a very large sum of money. So, deciding to take steps to conceal the affair, you persuaded Glynne—I imagine the suggestion came from you, though perhaps I'm wrong there—to get engaged to Marion Teed. You knew that Marion was in love with him. What, I suppose, you didn't realise was that Marion knew he was in love with you. She accepted him because —well, she herself can tell you, if she wants to, why she accepted him."

" I accepted him," said Marion, " because I was a fool and gave in to a fool's hope. But I understood almost at once why he'd asked me to marry him, and that was why I insisted on its being kept secret. But he got me to say he could tell Katharine, and Katharine told everyone."

" Exactly," I said. " A secret engagement would've been no use to them; the whole point was that the engagement should be known of; its function was simply to explain Glynne's visits up here. He and Mrs Peach between them took care that everyone knew of it; he even brought Miss Teed to sit outside my window last night, and talked, in a voice I couldn't fail to hear, about the engagement, to make sure that I should know about it without his seeming to go out of his way to tell me. He also took the opportunity then to throw some suspicion on Miss Teed for the killing of the chimpanzee by directing the conversation so as to let me know that she'd got a kind of jealousy-motive. This morning he made certain that this idea had got into my head by explaining to me that there was certainly no truth in such a supposition." I turned to Marion Teed again. "Glynne's treated you treacherously and rottenly," I said, "and about as callously as I've known a man treat a woman. He might even have treated you violently if he'd managed to get past Dr Virag on the stairs just now. He knew it must be you who found Miss Miall's handbag . . . now, won't you tell me the truth about where you found the bag?"

"But I've told you the truth," she replied.

"No," I said.

"I have!"

"You found that bag in Glynne's car while you sat waiting for him outside the Warrells' cottage. I suppose it had got jammed in a corner so that he overlooked it when he put Miss Miall into her grave. You found it, and your mind must already have been full of suspicions, because you weren't long in understanding its significance. In the clash of your loyalty to Miss Miall and your love for Glynne, it's easy to see which won, for your one thought was to hide the bag. But after that you didn't want to see Glynne again, so you ran away. Isn't that the truth?"

Her lips tightened.

I shrugged and went on: "Yesterday evening Mrs Peach and Glynne were in here together. Everyone else was out, hunting for the chimpanzees. Then in walked Miss Miall, and interrupted—well, I don't know what she interrupted, but it must have been enough to loosen up all her censoriousness. And as her tongue lashed at them, Mrs Peach's slender intelligence and self-control snapped under the strain. I hope when she comes to trial the judge will remember she had a drunken father and a mentally-deficient mother—soft-headed, as Sergeant Sawbry put it. Anyway, it was she who snatched the revolver out of the desk and fired."

"But . . . But . . ." Katharine Peach almost choked. "But it all makes such absolute nonsense! Why, I *couldn't* have done it! Even if I'd ever thought of such a thing—which, of course, I didn't, because I was absolutely devoted to Aunt Rosa, and quite naturally too, because she'd done absolutely everything for me—I simply couldn't have done it! I've got an *alibi*!"

"You've an excellent alibi for the death of Irma," I said, "but not for the death of Miss Miall, which may have happened as much as a quarter of an hour before Irma's. The first thing Glynne thought of when he saw what you'd done was to get you away from the place. He sent you down to the village by the path over the hill so that you couldn't be seen from the road, and he told you to make sure someone noticed you in East Leat. You followed his instructions. But as usual you went too far. You always went too far and said too much. When you brought out the bottle of whisky at supper you took pains to rub it in that you'd got an alibi; you took pains to tell me that Glynne disapproved of you; you tried to throw suspicion on your husband, Percy Peach, by telling me how much he hated Miss Miall; you took pains to point out to me that, since Dr Virag was to get his money in any case, you yourself could have no motive for killing Irma. You took pains to be altogether too innocent."

"But I *am* innocent!"

"No, Mrs Peach—because if you'd been innocent you'd never have dared to buy a bottle of whisky in the village and then produce it in the dining-room. Just as the vicar here didn't smoke in this room until after he'd heard Miss Miall was dead, you'd never have produced that bottle of whisky if there'd been the faintest risk of Miss Miall walking in and finding it."

"But you're making all this up out of nothing, nothing, nothing!" With her unbandaged hand she hammered the arm of her chair. "It's all talk, it's all nonsense, it doesn't mean anything! How d'you know what I'd dare do, or why I told you things, or—or how d'you know that Kenneth and I were in love? You haven't any proof of it! It's just that you've been listening to horrible gossip. You haven't any proof at all!"

"I think I have," I said.

"You haven't—you can't have!"

I walked towards her. "I have, Mrs Peach, and it won't take long to show you. Let me take that bandage off your hand."

She shrank back in her chair.

"My—bandage? Why?"

I realised as I drew near that she was trembling all over. I wondered how much longer her nerve would hold.

"Because under that bandage," I said, "I believe there's nothing but sound flesh. That bandage, like Marion Teed's engagement, was part of the plan to disguise your intimacy with Glynne. Even though he was supposed to be engaged to Marion, he could have time alone with you while he was dressing your hand. Now, if you don't mind——" I picked up her hand and started to unwind the bandage.

She drew away from me as far as she could while I was doing it. She looked small and crushed in the high-backed chair. Her eyes, it seemed to me, looked a little crazed. All the others were leaning forward to watch.

Suddenly, as the last layer of bandage came away, Katharine Peach burst into laughter. It was a hideous cackle of laughter, wild with hysteria.

I felt my face go red.

The long, slim hand that lay in mine was horribly swollen and coloured purple and green—a poisoned hand if ever I saw one.

I suppose I have got into the habit of relying too

246

much on George, and when he lets me down I flounder helplessly. It had been George's idea that I should lead up to that stripping away of the bandage. We had both been certain that the hand was uninjured. I had followed our plan in every detail, beginning with getting rid of Glynne. We knew the slenderness of the case against Katharine Peach, and had agreed that with Glynne there to guide her she might very likely steer safely past the dangerous spots. Glynne had gone with rather less persuasion than I had expected; perhaps the ordeal in the wood, when he had had to shovel into the earth the stout, battered body of an old woman, after his all-night struggle for the life of Jessie Warrell and her child, had altered his sense of values. Plainly he had been grateful for the chance of escape. But where had it all got me? There was no fake about Katharine Peach's poisoned hand. George's plan had let me down completely.

Mrs Peach had controlled her laughter.

"D'you know, I feel rather queer," she said faintly. "I think it's the shock of poor Aunt Rosa's death. I wonder if you'd mind fetching me a glass of water?"

Very nearly I went to fetch it. But just then I heard a laugh at my elbow.

"Poor Mr Dyke," said Marti Virag, "you are looking so very puzzled. You are always disbelieving people and then finding you are wrong in your disbelief. You are really very unfortunate."

"Marti, be quiet!" said her father.

"But I am so sorry for him, papa," said the girl,

" he stands there looking so helpless, and all the time it's so easy, if he only knew."

" Be quiet," said her father again, " this has nothing to do with you."

Her dark eyes went rebellious. She turned on Katharine Peach.

" Yes, it is quite simple! I've heard you say, Mrs Peach, and I've heard other people say that your cuts fester every time you cut yourself. I suppose that was why last Sunday—the day we got here— last Sunday in the evening, when I was walking in the garden and looked in at the window of this room, I saw Mrs Peach cutting herself with a pair of scissors. I suppose she likes having a poisoned hand! She was poking the point of her scissors into her hand in several places, and laughing——"

Katharine Peach was on her feet. " Oh, you liar! " she gasped. " You horrible little liar! "

" I'm not a liar! " cried Marti. " It is the truth. I never tell lies."

Katharine Peach appealed to all of us: " She's a terrible liar—you know she is. She can't help telling lies; that's the kind of person she is."

Virag gripped his daughter by the shoulder.

" Marti, are you lying? "

" No, no, I'm not! " she cried.

" She is! " screamed Katharine Peach.

" Marti," said Virag, " I know you are a liar, and I know it is much my fault because I have not been a wise father to you, but now we go to America as you wish, and I try to make things so it shall be better—but I tell you, if you are lying now I shall go to Greenland and devote myself to studying the mentality of the walrus for the rest of my life, and you shall live there with me."

"I'm not lying!" sobbed the girl. "I'm telling the truth. I saw her."

"Then why," I asked irritably, "didn't you say anything about it before?"

"Because I thought she was mad," said Marti sullenly. "With mad people one must be very kind and understanding. I thought everyone here was mad."

The expressionless voice of Marion Teed joined in: "She's probably telling the truth. Katharine's done things like that before. At first she kept making herself sick to get Kenneth up here. She's very—thorough."

"Probably, probably!" cried Katharine scornfully. "Is a jury going to listen, is anyone going to listen to what's *probably* true? You can't prove anything against me. You can't even prove Aunt Rosa was killed here. You can't prove there were any bloodstains. The carpet's gone to the cleaner's!" She began to laugh again. "It was your own friend who took it to the cleaner's—your own silly, little, fat friend. Isn't it funny? I said I was going to see to it, and he offered to take it himself. Your own friend, Mr Dyke!" She let out more wild peals of laughter.

That screaming laughter had a curious effect on us all; I could see it convinced everyone there of her guilt. But it had an effect I should not have foreseen on one member of the company who had taken no part in the discussion. Leofric had the usual animal dread and distrust of human laughter; as those peals rang out, suddenly and completely the chimpanzee lost his temper.

There was no question now of waving pieces of bamboo and taking up threatening attitudes. A compact, black ball of fury, he sprang.

Katharine Peach shrieked.

Virag and Ingham together leapt on the animal and caught him, but as they did so Katharine Peach acted swiftly in her own defence. She snatched at the crocodile-skin handbag on the mantelpiece, and as Ingham jerked Leofric back, Percy Peach's revolver barked twice.

The shots crashed harmlessly into the ceiling, for I had knocked her hand up.

"Thanks, Mrs Peach," I said. "I thought if I left the handbag there you'd do that sooner or later. But I wonder how you knew the revolver was there unless you were in the room when Kenneth Glynne put it into the bag?"

"That's right," came in George's placid voice from the doorway, "I reckon that proves she was there. And, by the way, about the carpet. It's quite true I took it to the cleaner's, because I knew if I didn't somebody else would, and I brought back a receipt so's everyone would feel sure I'd taken it. But the receipt only said 'one carpet'—it didn't say nothin' about an underfelt, and the underfelt with two good splotches of blood on it is upstairs in my suitcase under my bed. When some clever chemist gets to work on it, I reckon he'll be able to prove that one splotch of blood is a chimpanzee's and the other a human being's."

* * * * *

The police arrived a minute or so later. They brought some information. Kenneth Glynne had just been found unconscious in his surgery. He had injected morphine. There was no chance of his recovery.

When she knew it Marion Teed admitted she had found the handbag in his car. Katharine Peach was arrested.

That evening George and I had a talk with Virag. I got George to tell Virag how he had arrived at the truth.

"You see," said George, "it all came out of tryin' to find an explanation for the shape of the stain of blood. The idea about Irma bein' moved didn't seem to get us anywhere. And then I remembered the very first thing Tobe said when he bent over her as she lay there. 'And bled enough for two!' he said. For two! And then all the rest followed, because if someone else has bled there it couldn't very well be anyone but Rosa Miall, because no one else seemed to be missin'. But if it was her, then somehow or other her body had been got away, and there wasn't nothin' it could've been got away in but Dr Glynne's car. And then it turned out he hadn't been tellin' the truth about when he came up the hill. . . . See, it was all simple. But if anyone

251

any time tells you Toby Dyke ain't a great detective, you tell 'em about this case; you tell 'em about the way he just took one look at the corpse of the chimp, then hit the nail right on the head."

"Thank you, George," I said. "But all the same, I'm glad the case is concluded. I took a dislike to this neighbourhood the moment I got out of the train and saw that half-witted porter watering his flowers. And certainly, though I regret it now, I took a dislike to Rosa Miall. When I think of her as I saw her then, striding along ahead of us——"

"As you *saw* her?" said Virag, turning on me sharply. "You have *seen* Rosa Miall?"

"Oh yes," I said, "she arrived at Bule by the same train as we did. The porter was too busy with his flowers to collect her ticket. She marched out ahead of us and collared the only taxi. That left nothing in the whole of Bule for George and me to travel by but a hearse that couldn't be converted into a landaulette. . . . And I feel that in that thought there's a certain irony."